THE OLD FLAME

Written with A. P. Herbert's characteristic wry humour and great sense of fun...

Robin Moon finds Phyllis rather a distraction in the Sunday morning service – after all her golden hair does seem to shine rather more brightly than the Angel Gabriel's heavenly locks. His wife, Angela, on the other hand, is more preoccupied with the cavalier Major Trevor than perhaps she should be during the Litany. When, after an admirable pot-luck Sunday lunch, Robin descends to the depths of mentioning what happened on their honeymoon, the result is inevitable. Finding his independence once more, Robin links up with Phyllis and her friends and dabbles in some far from innocent matchmaking...

THE OLD FLAME

THE OLD FLAME

by

A. P. Herbert

Dales Large Print Books
Long Preston, North Yorkshire,
BD23 4ND, England.

British Library Cataloguing in Publication Data.

Herbert, A. P.
The old flame.

A catalogue record of this book is
available from the British Library

ISBN   978-1-84262-653-5 pbk

Published in Large Print 2009 by arrangement with
M. T. Perkins, Polly M. V. R. Perkins and the Executors of the
Estate of Jocelyn Herbert,
care of A. P. Watt Literary, Film & Television Agents

Dales Large Print is an imprint of Library Magna Books Ltd.

Printed and bound in Great Britain by
T.J. (International) Ltd., Cornwall, PL28 8RW

'EACH OF US, I SUPPOSE, HAS AN OLD FLAME SMOULDERING IN A CORNER OF HIS HEART'

MR GLADSTONE

CONTENTS

CHAPTER 1

A Judicious Separation

Halfway through the second hymn I caught sight of Phyllis Fair. Phyllis Fair was looking bewitching at the lower end of a shaft of sunlight from the south window (at the other end was the Angel Gabriel). The Angel Gabriel looked holy but unsociable; Phyllis looked charming but not holy. She was not singing. She wore a little toque. Phyllis is fairly tall, and very slender, and she has greeny-brown eyes which twinkle at a man and slay him. Her hair is old gold. It is neither bobbed nor shingled, nor barnacled, nor ribbed, but grows as God intended. But on either side two clusters of it trespass on to her cheeks; and there, I swear, they are reflected. She had her mother on one side, and a young man on the other. She always has a young man on one side, and, when she is in church, she very often has her mother on the other. She caught my eye. She smiled. I bowed. She raised her eyes to heaven, and slightly depressed the corners of her mouth, a horrid thing to do at Matins. She then yawned. I placed my hand on my heart and continued to sing with genuine fervour

That such a small affliction
Should win so great a prize!

Phyllis Fair continued to catch my eye for a verse or two, and it may be that I continued to sing

That such a small affliction
Should win so great a prize!

At any rate, I found people looking hard at me, as people do at those who sing in church. I also found my dear wife Angela looking hard at Phyllis Fair.

And when we knelt down she whispered in one of her cold voices (she has three), 'So *that's* why you were so anxious to come to church?'

I replied, 'No, it wasn't. What do you mean?'

She said, 'You know what I mean.'

I said, 'Yes.' And I added casually, 'I see Major Trevor in the north transept.'

(It's no good telling me that decent

married people don't go on like this during the Litany – they do.)

Angela has a ridiculous habit of blushing; still more ridiculous, she is ashamed of it. I like it. When I said that I saw Major Trevor in the north transept, Angela blushed, and began praying.

I turned my eyes towards Major Trevor; for Phyllis was praying too. And the Major quickly looked the other way.

There is a well-established theory that I am not a jealous man. Nor am I. Nonetheless, it baffles me to see what a decent, intelligent woman can see in a man like the Major. Well-groomed, I know; but so are racehorses. Well set-up, yes; but so is a policeman. A VC; but I too have a certain courage, both physical and moral – chiefly moral.

The truth is, the man is *passionate*. And he is heroic. The last time he invited Angela to run away with him, he said things which would have brought the Lyceum down in ruins on the auditorium. And the best of women like a change, now and then.

And, I must admit, the man amuses *me*.

We found the Major talking to the Fair party in the churchyard.

'Darling!' said Angela, as she kissed Phyllis.

'How sweet you look!' said Phyllis, as she kissed Angela. 'My dear, where *did* you get that duck of a hat? Rachel Slade has one just like it.'

'No doubt, by this time,' said Angela, coolly. 'I've worn this a fortnight. Well, Major, I didn't know you ever went to church.'

'I don't,' said the idiot, with a gallant bow; and seeing that Angela was about to blush, I turned, in sheer compassion, to Phyllis and the new young man.

'Good morning, John,' said Phyllis. (I don't know *why* she calls me John; it is not my name, and I am not that sort of man.) 'Good morning, John. Do you know Mr Gordon Smith?'

'No,' I murmured. 'I thought I knew them all. How do you do, Mr Smith?'

'How do you do?' said Mr Smith. 'I've heard so much about you.'

'Then please don't repeat it,' I said. 'It's not true.'

Mr Smith shook hands shyly, and melted into the background in a very proper manner.

'I want you to like him,' said Phyllis. 'And you've frightened him away.'

'I hardly looked at him.'

'Exactly,' said Phyllis. 'He's nice,' she added.

'Then I don't like him.' I took a good look at the young man, who was undoubtedly nice, very young, very clean-shaven, very smooth-skinned and brown. 'No, I don't like him at all. Well, well, I hope he'll be very happy.'

'Not *me?*' said Phyllis, with what she thinks is a pout.

'It's not necessary to hope that.'

'I don't know. I felt quite sad in church.'

'So did I,' I said. 'It was the second hymn that upset me.'

'The *second* hymn?'

'The one about the small affliction and the great prize.'

'I don't remember that,' said Phyllis.

'I don't think you sang it.'

'Ah!' said Phyllis, with a faint flush. 'You should keep your eyes from picking and stealing, Mr Moon.'

'In church, Miss Fair? I don't remember—'

'*Now,* Mr Moon. I ought to tell you that I'm very nearly engaged.'

'I'm not surprised,' I said. 'You were very nearly married once.'

'Twice,' said Phyllis, softly.

'I don't count the other one. Never did.'

'Which do you mean by the *other* one?'

'Poor Stephen,' I sighed. 'He never suited you.'

'I never saw,' said Phyllis, lightly, 'much difference between them. Come along, Gordon; we mustn't be late for lunch. I'm sorry you can't lunch with us, Mr Moon.'

'I can,' I said, 'if I'm asked.'

'There isn't enough for another,' said Phyllis, with a little laugh – a little self-conscious laugh, I thought.

'I don't want much,' I said. 'But I like watching. You see, I've lunched already, in a manner of speaking. Just a course or two – the *hors-d'oeuvre.*'

Mr Smith regarded me with round brown eyes.

'Don't look so stupefied, Gordon,' said Phyllis. 'Mr Moon's an author; and they never know what they're saying.'

'But we generally know what other people are doing,' I remarked. 'Goodbye, Mr Smith. I hope you'll be happy, I'm sure.'

'What does he mean *now?*' The young man gurgled.

'Goodbye, John,' said Phyllis. 'You ought to be ashamed of yourself.'

'Well, some people don't *like* lunch – and have it thrown at them. And some people don't appreciate a good lunch when they see it. And some people–'

But they had gone.

The Major likes lunch, of *course*.

'Well, goodbye, Major,' I said, cheerfully.

He said, 'Ha! Your wife very kindly said something about a spot of lunch. Pot-luck. Ha!'

It is a curious thing; Major Trevor has eaten many elaborate meals at my house, but neither Angela nor I have ever invited him to anything but a 'spot of lunch', and he has never accepted anything but 'pot-luck'. We never ask anyone else to have a 'spot of lunch'; I cannot think where we picked up the horrid phrase. But the Major is one of those Englishmen to whom one feels it is impossible to speak the King's English.

'First-rate,' I said. ('First-rate!') 'There's enough, I suppose, Angela?'

'Oh, plenty!' said Angela, brightly.

'Ha! I don't want anything,' said the Major. (I wish these military men would not explode so.) 'Pot-luck, you know. Bread and cheese. Do me fine.'

'There's no cheese, I *know*,' I said. 'Have we any bread, my dear?'

'Plenty,' said Angela, less brightly.

'Then that's all right. It's all right about the

servants, I suppose?' I went on, anxiously.

'Of *course* it's all right,' said Angela, tapping her foot on the ground.

'Don't let me be a nuisance, old fellow,' said the Major.

'Certainly not, old man. No, I only thought it was Mary's day out, and as a rule my wife doesn't like to give her too much washing-up on her day out. But I suppose it's her day in today, Angela?'

'No,' said Angela, shortly. 'But one makes no difference.'

'Not if he's only going to eat bread, of course,' I said, cheerily. 'Well, that's all right, old fellow. Let's get along then.'

We got along.

During lunch the Major behaved in a very ridiculous fashion. Mind you, I *like* the fellow, and I suppose that a VC has a certain duty to be gallant; but, in my opinion, an excess of gallantry in the guest of a married couple is very bad manners. When Angela was called to the telephone during the meal I consider it was bad manners on the Major's part to leap to his feet and ostentatiously open the door for her. Angela is very able to open a door for herself; she has had years of training in opening doors for herself – five years. But I could see that she enjoyed it.

20

Then why must he keep on *passing* her things? It must have been evident to him, as it was to me, that Angela had everything she could possibly desire – meat, vegetables, sauce, bread, water, and condiments. But he kept on passing her things. And I could see that Angela enjoyed it. When he had offered her everything on the table, and most of the things twice, he rose and fetched the sauce-cruet from the sideboard.

'Worcester sauce, Mrs Moon?' he said, charmingly.

I happen to know that Angela loathes Worcester sauce, and I have long ago ceased to offer her Worcester sauce. I don't offer her mustard, for the same reason.

'Thank you, Major,' said Angela, with a grateful look, and she poured a quantity on her potato.

These women!

The Major sat down, with the satisfied air of a man who has brought a ray of happiness into the life of a neglected woman. And Angela looked very much the same.

'Won't you have a little mustard, my dear?' I said, solicitously, passing the pot.

'No, thank you, dear,' said Angela, sweetly, pushing it away. 'You *know* I don't like mustard.'

Meanwhile, the Major ate a great deal.

A little later he said, 'I hope you'll give us a little music afterwards, Mrs Moon?'

'Afraid not,' said Angela, sighing. 'I don't play nowadays. I've scarcely *touched* a piano these last few years – since I was married,' she concluded.

'Pity,' said the Major, warmly. 'Let me get you another spot of beef,' and he rushed to the sideboard. 'Oh, but you ought to keep up your music,' he went on, carving busily.

'You won't persuade her, Major,' I said. 'Not now she's married. Nothing kills a woman's music like marriage. You remember that, Major, if you ever have a musical daughter. What was it you were trying to practise yesterday, Angela? One of the old things, wasn't it?'

'I was strumming,' said Angela.

'Strumming?' I protested. 'I remember you playing me that piece when we were engaged, my dear – hour after hour. I loved it. I'm afraid she won't play it to you, Major.'

'Do, now,' said the Major, returning with a heap of beef. 'I'm not musical, you know,' as if the whole world suspected him of music.

'Oh, well, if the Major's not particular,' said Angela, 'perhaps I might.'

'Ah!' said I. 'Won't you have a little mustard now, my dear?'

'Pretty girl, that Miss Fair,' said the Major, after a pause.

'Yes,' said Angela, without passion. 'She's a very old friend of Robin's' (for that is my real name, and not John).

'You don't like her?' said the Major, in his delicate way.

'She's nice,' said Angela, judicially. 'But I don't feel there's anything *in* her. Do you?'

This phrase does not occur in books and melodramas, but it is, in fact, the most awful thing that one woman can say of another.

'A deep one, I should say,' the Major ventured.

'I shouldn't wonder,' said Angela, darkly.

Since Angela and I became man and wife I have never yet liked any lady who was not both wholly lacking in anything 'in her', and at the same time desperately deep. In fact, every nice young lady of my acquaintance is, as far as I can judge, an unfathomable pit, both shallow and deep, stuffed with wicked designs, and absolutely empty.

'I think, perhaps, you had better play to us now,' I said, 'that thing you used to play when we were engaged, my dear. The Major will like that.'

Angela played very charmingly for about an hour, and the Major let his cigar go out. About four he went away.

'Promised to take a dish of tea at Hampstead,' he explained.

'Pot-luck, I suppose?' I said.

At about 4.15 Angela developed one of her sighing fits.

'I wish we could find some nice girl for Bim,' she said at last (that is the creature's preposterous name – Major Bim Trevor).

'Why a *nice* girl?' I said.

'He'd make such a good husband. He's so considerate.'

'He isn't a husband.'

'Everybody isn't like you,' said Angela.

'Who is?' I said, humbly. 'I'm like nobody on earth, I know. Wasn't that why you married me?'

'No,' said Angela, warmly. 'I thought you were a normal human being, instead of – instead of–' And, finding no words, she threatened a tear.

'You said at the time, I remember,' I said, reflectively, 'that I was so different from everybody else.'

'You're certainly the *oddest* man I ever

knew,' said Angela, forgetting about crying.

'Well, well. How would Phyllis do for the Major? She's got nothing in her, and he has everything. What a match!'

'How your mind runs on that girl!'

'Another of my oddities. My friends used to say it was odd I never married; but when I married it was odder still; then you used to say it was odd I would never take any notice of the nice young women you had to the house, and *now* it's odd if I look at one.'

'Well, it *is* odd. You never used to. I haven't forgotten that Burberry girl.'

'*I* have. Who was she?'

'The yellow-haired one.'

'Her name was Marbury. And her hair was pure gold.'

'Oh, yes!' sniffed Angela. 'Like Phyllis'.'

'Nothing like Phyllis'. How your mind runs on that girl!'

'Not at all,' said Angela, haughtily. 'But I know one thing – if it had been Phyllis called to the 'phone you'd have opened the door for her.'

'I know another thing. If it had been Phyllis the Major wouldn't have opened the door.'

'Yes, he would.'

'Very well, my dear. You're right, of course.'

'It's no good,' said Angela. 'You've never looked after me properly, not even' – and producing a handkerchief the size of a stamp she prepared to staunch the threatening tear – 'not even on my – my h – h – *honeymoon.*'

A tear fell.

'You've never been reasonable,' I replied – 'not even on *my* honeymoon. *I* haven't forgotten how you sulked from Friday to Tuesday at Caddenabia.'

(I am sorry; but this is how one does talk, now and then.)

'Oh, oh! – how *can* you?' said Angela. All the tears fell; and I melted.

'I am sorry,' I said. 'I'll go and pack.'

About once in every two years Angela and I, like other couples, arrive at a stage when a month's separation would clearly be the best thing for us. Unlike others, we take it. Angela calls it the 'Rest-Cure.' I call it the 'Holiday Moon.' When the moment comes we never want to take it. But this, we know, is weakness, and we have sworn to resist it; and a long time ago we made certain definite rules to fortify us. One of these rules is that when Angela goes back to what I did on her honeymoon (to this day I have never discovered what it was) the moment is approaching; and if on the same day I go back to the 'Great Sulk' the moment has come. The rule then is Instant Action.

However, it *is* hard.

'Yes,' said Angela, through her tears, 'you're quite right. Go on.'

'No, no,' said I, preparing to take the creature in my arms. 'Let's try again. I was horrid.'

'It's no good,' said she, pushing me away. 'You know the rules. It will only be the same thing tomorrow. Go on,' she said. 'I was a beast,' and she wept again.

I went and packed, miserable.

When I came down Angela was busy with a Bradshaw, miserable.

'Where will you go?' I said.

'I shall go to Margaret's,' said Angela, sadly.

'I shall go to the club,' I said, dismally. 'There's my taxi. Goodbye, my dear,' and we embraced very tenderly.

'Oh, Robin, *must* we–?' said Angela, clinging.

I wavered. 'No,' I said. And then I remembered that it is the duty of the man to be strong. 'Yes,' I said, 'we've got to go through with it. Goodbye, my darling.'

'Goodbye, my pet.'

'I'll send on your washing,' said Angela.

'I'll send you a cheque,' said I.

'Take care of yourself,' we both said, tenderly.

'The taxi's waiting,' said Elizabeth.

CHAPTER 2

Thick Or Clear

As I have already hinted, my dear wife Angela and I, being a man and woman of the human race, arrive now and then at a stage in our relations when we feel that if we live together a moment longer we shall scream. But being unusually sensible members of the human race we do not scream; neither do we elope to Italy with others: we do not even throw things about. But we make a judicious separation of a month and take a holiday from each other. This does not happen often. In five years of matrimony this was only our third Holiday Moon; and many more orthodox couples are married, divorced, and remarried twice over in the same period. The rules are simple but severe. The statutory period is a month (to be extended to two on either party desiring it – in writing; but I may say that there has never yet been a two-monthly Moon); and once the Moon is embarked upon no weakening is allowed. However much we may long to be reunited after the first week, the Moon must be completed; this is of the essence of the cure.

On the same principle neither of us is allowed to live at home. Angela goes to friends and sisters and so on; I go to the club. If we happen to meet, we meet, so far as possible, as strangers. To make this easier Angela reverts to her stage name (for I have to confess that Angela was, and sometimes is still, an actress); and during a Moon I have once or twice been introduced to my wife, which is fun. As to conduct, we expect each other to behave ourselves, within reasonable limits, and any action which may reasonably be regarded as an indiscretion must be reported at the close of the Moon. Most of our friends know about our system, and most of them regard us as mad. Perhaps we are. And perhaps we are the only sane couple in the Kingdom.

As I say, I go to the club. And to the club I went, a melancholy man, the first evening of the third Holiday Moon.

I loathe my club. I only go there as part of the tradition. The club is the traditional shrine of man's independence, and every married man is supposed to fly to it, as to a haven, at the first opportunity. In cold fact, I believe that every married man is as heartily bored by his club as I am.

Still, it is the obvious place in which to make a fine gesture of independence, and I steeled myself to make the most of it. I dumped my luggage in the comfortable, horrible bachelor austerity of Bedroom No.4, and looked out of the window. The window looks on to four chimneys, a slate roof, and an exceedingly high wall.

'Good Lord!' I said. And then again, 'Good Lord!'

But this would never do.

'Freedom,' I whispered, manfully. 'Freedom! Independence!'

I went down to dinner. And I took a book with me. For the real argument against marriage is that it cuts you off from reading at meals.

I sat down at a nice corner table, propped my book against the water-jug, and began, I must say, to feel free and independent. No one disturbed me, no one expected me to talk; not even a waiter approached me. I read a chapter.

Then I looked up and saw a fresh, clean-shaven young man hovering in my direction, as if uncertain whether it was safe to grin at me. He took the risk, and grinned. I recognized him then as the new young man I had met at church with Phyllis Fair – in all probability the man who was about to link his life with Phyllis Fair's. I was interested. I am always interested in the men who are about to link their lives with Phyllis Fair's.

'Gordon Smith,' I said, shaking hands.

'You don't remember me,' he said, foolishly.

'Then you're not Mr Smith?'

'Yes,' he said, grinning.

'Then I *do* remember you.'

'Yes,' he said. 'But I thought perhaps you'd forgotten me.'

(It is extraordinary the time and trouble the human race devotes to little conversations of this kind.)

'No,' I said, 'I never forget Phyllis Fair's friends. Phyllis does, sometimes,' I added. 'Come and dine.'

'Oh, but aren't you expecting somebody?'

'No.'

'You're sure I shan't be in the way?'

'Not quite,' I said, thinking of Phyllis. 'That's what I want to find out. Sit down.'

'You do say funny things,' said Mr Smith,

sitting down cautiously.

'That's my profession. They don't mean anything. You mustn't mind me. I'm feeling very independent tonight.'

'Thick or clear, Mr Moon?' said Paragon, the head waiter.

I studied the menu. Artichoke soup – delicious; and *consommé du ciel* – delicious.

'Both,' I said, grandly.

'Certainly, sir,' said Paragon, not moving a muscle.

'And I shall have both kinds of fish, no entrée, both savouries, and no sweet. A half-bottle of Burgundy, and a half-bottle of Sauterne. I *will* be free.'

'Certainly, sir,' said Paragon. 'And which soup will you be taking first, Mr Moon?'

'The artichoke, Paragon; for that is a thing of solid worth, which I shall consume and enjoy. Then I shall find fault with it and wish I had had the thin first. But being no longer in a position to enjoy the thin (for no man can consume *two* soups, Paragon) I shall do no more than toy with it, as with an unattainable dream. And since I shall not consume it, I shall always think of it as better than the thick. It will remain a dream. Soup, Paragon, is very like love.'

'Yes, sir,' said Paragon, and went away.

'Are you in love, Mr Smith?' I continued, politely.

'To tell you the truth–' Mr Smith began, cautiously.

'I was hoping you'd tell me that.'

'I believe I am,' he said, looking very hot.

'Strange,' I said. 'In my experience either a man is in love with Phyllis or he is not. She is that kind of girl. It *is* Phyllis, I suppose? I'm sorry for you.'

I was. Against my better judgment, I *liked* the young man; and I felt generously ready to give him good advice on the subject of marrying Phyllis; for that is a subject on which I so very nearly became an authority. I fancied I knew what the poor young man was suffering.

The young man nodded gloomily.

'She's one of them,' he said.

I was shocked.

'Do you mean to tell me,' I said, 'that you're not certain? About Phyllis?'

'About either of them,' said the shameless boy. 'The fact is – I wish you'd advise me, Mr Moon. The fact is' – he repeated earnestly – 'the fact is, *I believe I'm in love with two women. Is that possible?*' And, flushing, he buried his face in his soup.

'Really, my boy,' I said, severely, 'you

34

mustn't say things of that kind. Not in the club. I never heard of such a thing.'

Mr Smith looked piteous.

'I know,' he said, 'it's an awful thing to say. But – but – what you said about the two soups – I thought perhaps it *might* happen sometimes. I feel I'm a brute.'

'Oh, well, it's not quite as bad as that. There *have* been cases, I believe... After all, there *are* women who are very much alike... But Phyllis... Really...'

And, indeed, I felt much less generously disposed towards Mr Smith.

'She's wonderful, I know,' sighed Mr Smith. 'But I can't make up my mind.'

'Who is the other, may I ask? This soup is capital.'

'Jean Renton.' He sighed again.

The puppy! Jean Renton is dark and beautiful, I know; she is also only half awake. To compare her with Phyllis... I decided that Mr Smith had forfeited my sympathy. I decided also that I would teach him (painfully and slowly) to appreciate Phyllis.

'Jean has more soul, you find?' I suggested.

'Yes,' he said, looking away. 'I couldn't have expressed it myself; but, yes, that's what it is, I suppose. She's topping.'

'And such eyes?'

'Yes,' he said, eagerly. 'Wonderful eyes.'

'One feels,' I went on, as if searching for the exact phrase – 'one feels that there's something *in* her, doesn't one?'

'Yes,' he said. 'That's it!'

'And in cold fact there's nothing at all,' I thought – but I did not say this.

'Yes,' said the boy, becoming bold. 'That's what one feels about her – although she doesn't say much.'

'Having nothing to say,' I reflected.

The waiter brought my second plate of soup. 'Phyllis, on the other hand,' I went on, 'is lively enough–'

'Oh, yes, she's full of life.'

'And very pretty–'

'She's topping.'

'But somehow one doesn't feel' – and again I paused for the right phrase – 'one doesn't feel that there's so much *in* her – if you know what I mean.'

'That's what I mean, exactly,' said the youth, solemnly. 'A bit – what's the word? – *shallow.*'

The cub!

'My wife,' I did not say, 'considers that Phyllis is deep.'

'Those fair girls,' I did say, a little

meaninglessly, 'are very often the same.'

'All the same,' said Mr Smith, stoutly, 'she's terribly pretty.'

'Terribly,' I agreed. 'But, of course, it never lasts. Not that fair type. It's the old problem – Thick or Clear?'

'She's an awfully good sort,' said he.

The dog! 'A good sort,' indeed!

'That's true,' I said. 'Still, one doesn't marry "a good sort", does one?'

'No,' he sighed. 'I don't know *what* to do. What do *you* advise, Mr Moon?'

'Must you decide immediately?'

'Oh, well,' he said, 'I was twenty-four last week. I'm getting on, you know.'

'Time you were getting off, you mean?'

Mr Smith giggled kindly.

'My advice is this, my boy,' I said. 'Take your time about it. Take – well, take *a month,* shall we say? And during that month don't see too much of either of the ladies. *Think* about them as much as you like – think about them both – and see how you feel about them at a distance. Get them in perspective, so to speak; and then I fancy you'll see your way clear.'

(Nothing is more satisfactory than to do a bad action which at the same time you know to be good. I felt a warm glow steal over me.)

'I'm awfully grateful to you,' said the boy. 'I believe you're right – though, by gad, it will be hard.'

And he clenched his beautiful teeth.

'I know,' I said, with sympathy. 'I should say you were a very *passionate* man.'

'I suppose I am,' he said, modestly, toying with his sole.

'To be capable of passion,' I answered, gravely, 'is the great test of manhood. I have always envied those who–'

'Why,' said the young man, suddenly, 'you haven't touched your second plate of soup!'

'I'm afraid I never shall,' I replied, as Paragon removed it. 'I am incapable. All the same, I do appreciate it.'

'I wish I knew what you meant,' said Mr Smith.

'I'm glad you don't,' said I.

As soon after dinner as was decent I left Mr Smith in a profound study with a liqueur brandy in the smoking-room, and I rang up the house of Mrs Fair, a very good friend of mine.

A voice was heard like – like a very, very soft electric shock.

'Is that Miss Fair?' I said.

'That depends,' said the voice, cautiously.

'Is that you, Phyllis?' I said.

'No, Mr Moon,' said the voice. 'It's Miss Fair.'

'Are you doing anything tomorrow evening?'

'That depends, Mr Moon.'

'What does it depend on?'

'It depends who asks me, Mr Moon.'

'Suppose a gentleman asked you to dance with him.'

'I'm supposing that. I thought of dancing with Mr Smith.'

'I've just been talking to him. He didn't say anything about it.'

'He doesn't know yet,' said Phyllis.

'Ah!' I said. 'How is your mother?'

'She's asleep – in an armchair.'

'And what are you doing, Miss Fair?'

'I thought, perhaps, Mr Smith might call. He very often calls on Sundays. We play backgammon.'

'Mr Smith is asleep,' I said – 'in an armchair.'

'How very rude!'

'Hold on a moment,' I said, and I skipped lightly from the box, and peeped into the smoking-room; for I have a conscience, like the rest of us.

'Yes,' I said, returning to the box, 'Mr Smith is asleep – in the same armchair.'

'Extraordinary!'

'I can't understand it.'

'I think you said you'd been talking to him, Mr Moon.'

There was a pause.

'*I* can play backgammon,' I said at last.

There was no answer.

'Supposing a gentleman called–' I began.

There was no answer.

In the smoking-room Mr Smith still slept. The puppy!

'Don't mind mother,' said Phyllis, a little later. 'She doesn't *mean* to snore. Or would you rather I woke her up?'

'Don't bother,' I said. 'Not on my account. Will you throw first, Phyllis?'

'Thank you, John.'

'Why *do* you call me John?' I said.

'You're so respectable, Mr Moon. I always think of a married man as John. Two sixes! Just my luck!'

'Two ones,' said I. 'Just mine!'

The game continued.

'Are you going to marry Mr Smith?' I said, politely, at the third throw.

'Mother snores like this every evening,' said Phyllis, irrelevantly.

'Are you in love with Mr Smith?' I said.

'He has a car,' said Phyllis, lightly.

'He is asleep,' I said.

'That might happen to any man.'

'It didn't happen to me.'

'Perhaps your conscience, Mr Moon–'

'Stephen had a car too,' I went on. Stephen is the man to whom Phyllis was (till recently) engaged.

'What do you mean by that, John?'

'I'm afraid the noise of the dice may disturb your mother,' I said. 'Let's put them away.'

'Yes,' said Phyllis. 'It's a silly game.'

'I'd like to tell you about a story I'm writing,' I said.

'A sad story, John?'

'A sad story, Phyllis.'

'Good! I'm feeling sad.'

'It's about a girl and a man – a man called John. The girl was very much in love with him–'

'How do you know that?' said Phyllis, fiddling with her back hair, and therefore showing the line of her neck, which is a good line.

'That's the story.'

'Oh!'

'But he, being a bit of an ass, was too frightened to propose to her – kept putting

41

it off. And one day another man proposed to her. He had a Rolls Royce,' I added.

'Go on,' said Phyllis, a thought impatiently.

'And she accepted him. And then the first man, being a bit of an ass, just gave it up and married somebody else. And after that the girl – one can't blame her, in a way–'

'No,' said Phyllis, generously.

'The girl behaved as if she didn't much *care*. As long as they had cars... She was engaged to various makes in her times. The second was a Singer–'

'A silly story,' said Phyllis. 'And what's the end of it?'

'It isn't finished yet,' I said. 'I'm not quite clear how it will work out. But I hope she'll turn sensible before the end.'

'I'm afraid you're rather sentimental, Mr Moon,' said Phyllis.

'I'm afraid I am.'

Just then the door opened and the butler entered stealthily.

'Mr Smith has called,' he said.

'Oh, dear!' said Phyllis, going a little pink. 'I don't think I'm At Home. Am I At Home, Mr Moon?'

'It depends,' I said.

'No,' said Phyllis, looking at her mother,

'we're not at home, Lavery.'

A few moments later dear old Mrs Fair woke up with a start.

'Hullo, Mr Moon!' she said. 'What's that noise? It quite frightened me.'

'It sounds like a car,' I said, 'going away.'

'It sounds like a Singer,' said Phyllis.

CHAPTER 3

The Whisper

Whoever it was, it cannot be denied that he (and she, for that matter) did wrong.

The Whispering Gallery at St Paul's Cathedral is an interesting place, and has interesting properties. An ascent of one hundred and forty-three steps leads to an open door on the right by which entry is gained to a gallery (the triforium) leading westward over the south nave aisle to the library. But we did not go to the library.

A strangely assorted party. A deplorably frivolous party. Phyllis, whom you know; and myself, whom you know; and Mr Gordon Smith, whom you know; and Stephen Trout, and Jean Renton.

Young Mr Gordon Smith, as I have hinted, is determined to marry Phyllis Fair or Jean Renton, but does not know which; and, for reasons of my own, I have advised him not to be in a hurry for the next few weeks. Stephen Trout is a barrister, I am sorry to say, and was till recently engaged to Phyllis – or, as I prefer to put it, Phyllis was engaged to Stephen Trout's little car. Stephen is now determined to marry Jean Renton. And they all go about together in the most shameless fashion, as if nothing had happened. For that matter, nothing has happened. The question is, Will anything ever happen?

For Stephen Trout, though bold enough with judges, is a poltroon with women. I cannot imagine how he ever screwed himself to the point of proposing to Phyllis. I don't suppose he did. But no doubt Phyllis knows how it was done.

Jean Renton, on the other hand, will never do for him what Phyllis did for him (if she did). Jean is beautiful, and magnetic, but almost wholly asleep; she has great, brown, melancholy eyes, and it is generally considered that deep within her a powerful soul lies dormant. I do not know about the soul (nobody does), but there is no doubt about the lying dormant. She has a sleepy, far-away gaze, as if she was always in a distant dream – a dream which I believe to be about nothing at all. Not that she pretends it is. To pretend anything would be too much of an effort. She seldom reads. She never looks at a newspaper. She just exists, always agree-

able, always ready to do anything that anyone proposes, but perfectly incapable of
proposing any kind of action on her own
account. Why should she? for we all know
that she would just as soon sit down and do
nothing at all. Even when she laughs it is like
a sweet, sad protest – not against the joke,
but against the effort. And she, too, is shy.

So how Stephen Trout and she are ever to
be united has long been a puzzle. Meanwhile, of course, the dashing Mr Smith may
capture her instead.

It may be suggested that I, a married man,
judiciously separated from my wife for a
month, should have kept myself clear of
such a party. I indignantly deny the sug-
gestion. These young things want an older
head among them, and I can give the oldest
of them a couple of years. It is true I suffer
no positive discomfort in Phyllis Fair's
company, but I must not be thought to be
selfish. I am anxious that Jean Renton's soul
should be dug up somehow and handed
over to someone – preferably Stephen, I
think. I am anxious that Mr Smith should
make up his mind, but not too quickly; for I
question whether he and Phyllis are *really*
the right match. And I don't want Phyllis to
marry Mr Smith's car. I don't want her to

marry anybody's car.

And I do *not* see how all these things can be arranged without my assistance. Besides, they amuse me, the young things.

At any rate, we found ourselves, the five of us, feeding the pigeons in St Paul's Churchyard one lovely sunny noon. The pigeons of St Paul's on a sunny day are the most peaceful spectacle in London. East and west, the buses, and the taxis, and the lorries, and the drays thunder up and down the hill; and anxious clerks and city magnates scurry along the pavements, intent on doing something, or stopping somebody from doing something. And in the middle, the pigeons, whole regiments of them, strut and coo and stroll about on their own particular piece of pavement, remote and unconcerned; and a great crowd of Londoners stands near and watches them, having, apparently, no other thing in the world to do.

I stood near Phyllis, having, at the moment, no better thing in the world to do.

Phyllis wore a dress of almond-green, and Jean a black dress. Jean looked pale and noble, like a statue; but Phyllis looked a little pink and a little brown, like a shepherdess. And she looked the coolest thing in London. She is.

At first sight a crowd of pigeons look mean and unimportant and all alike, like men on the Underground; but, after a little, they become beautiful, and full of character, and, oh! so important.

'There's Stephen,' said Phyllis, at last, pointing at a pigeon with a neck of brown shot silk. He was pursuing assiduously a beautiful dark-blue pigeon, in and out among the other pigeons and the feet of the city men, his decorative head working backwards and forwards, absorbed, oblivious.

'You see?' said Phyllis. 'He is always exactly the same distance behind.'

'Just out of pecking distance.'

'But every now and then he makes a feeble peck at her.'

'And misses.'

'There, she's stopped to eat!'

But Stephen was too polite to peck while a lady was eating. He hovered dutifully at her side until she had finished, and hurried away; and then the relentless chase began again.

'It *is* Stephen!' cried Phyllis.

'S'sh! He'll hear you!'

'No, he won't. He's pecking.'

'As a matter of fact, he's merely hovering.'

And there, in fact, a little way away, was the handsome barrister, hovering at Jean's side – speechless and pathetic; and Jean Renton gazing at the pigeons – speechless and in trance, dreaming, I fancied, of the moment when she would sit down again.

'Can we do *nothing* about those two?' I said.

'What do you want to do?' said Phyllis.

'I should like to see them bring it off,' I said.

'I've noticed,' said Phyllis, 'that married men are strangely anxious to marry off your friends, Mr Moon.'

'Not all of them,' I murmured.

'Convicts, I believe, are never so happy as on the day when a new batch of prisoners arrive.'

'Not at all. The more ladies married the fewer temptations for us; the more men married the fewer rivals. Besides, we want to see our friends as happy as we are.'

'I am not sure,' said Phyllis, 'that you are *quite* the best authority on who should marry whom. There's Angela,' she said, irrelevantly.

The pigeon at which she pointed had no sort of resemblance to my wife, except that she was beautiful; she was standing alone, with a faintly peevish look, and at that moment two handsome pigeons, with necks like peacocks, approached her simultaneously, on which she instantly turned and ran away. The two pigeons followed.

'Nothing like,' I said. 'You're very rude.'

'Well,' said Phyllis, 'what are you going to do about those two?'

'Those two? Nothing,' I answered, haughtily.

'Jean and Stephen, I meant.'

'Oh! Well, unless Jean can be induced to run away, I'm afraid that Stephen will continue to hover.'

'She'll never run away,' said Phyllis. 'Too much trouble. Unless – Why shouldn't *you* take her in hand, Mr Moon? You never know – she might like you; she's a funny creature. You might make Stephen jealous. And then–'

'I've quite enough on my hands, thank you,' I said. 'All the same, I feel we ought to do *something*.'

The pigeons, for no apparent reason, rose suddenly into the air, with a multitudinous flapping, and, swinging out over the omnibuses, flew twice round the churchyard, a compact crowd, in a foolish affectation of panic. The spell of peacefulness was broken.

'Let's go up to the Whispering Gallery,' I said, for no apparent reason.

'Oh, yes!' said Phyllis. 'I love whispering. Let's ask the others if they'd like it.'

Phyllis asked the others if they'd like it in

characteristic fashion.

'Come on,' she said. 'We're all going up to the Whispering Gallery.'

'Very well,' said Jean, with her sad, sweet smile, as one agreeing to be burned alive for the general good.

Stephen had a pigeon perched on one hand and feeding out of the other. 'I was wondering,' said Stephen, who, like other barristers, talks 'law-shop' on the smallest provocation and looks upon Life as just another Leading Case, 'if I walked away with this pigeon, whether it would amount to a taking under the Larceny Act. The pigeon is not an animal *ferae naturae;* and nobody, as far as I know, has any property in the bird—'

'It belongs to the Dean of St Paul's,' said Phyllis, with authority.

'On the other hand—' said Stephen.

'Come and whisper it, old boy,' said Mr Smith, and we left the learned man still delivering judgment to the pigeon.

We paid our shillings, we laboured up one hundred and forty-three steps, and were joined by Stephen, panting, at the top.

'The visitor,' says the guide-book, 'presently reaches the Whispering Gallery, whose secrets he will learn by obeying the instruction of the guide in attendance.

Absolute quiet is essential, but, if silence is kept, the quietest whisper is distinctly audible.'

And if there be any blame for what followed it rests entirely with the Dean and Chapter of St Paul's. The guide in attendance greeted us with a broad grin, and it was clear that he at least regarded the Gallery as a place of entertainment. Having paid our shillings, we were ready to be entertained.

We looked down to the distant floor, and up to the distant dome, and marvelled reverently.

'Now,' said the guide, when he thought we had marvelled enough, 'if you will walk round to the other side the secrets of the Gallery will be revealed.'

'It will be more fun,' I said, 'if we split up.'

Accordingly, we set off in the dim light round the vast circle – Jean and Stephen one way, the rest of us the other – and halted, one by one, at different points: Stephen, as it were, at eight o'clock, Jean at eleven, myself at one, then Mr Smith, then Phyllis.

And suddenly a compelling, mysterious whisper smote me in the ear: 'SIT DOWN!'

I sat down, as if struck, and, looking across, observed our guide with his nose glued to the wall.

'PLEASE PLACE THE EARS TO THE WALL,' was the next order.

I placed as many of my ears to the wall as I conveniently could, and listened eagerly.

Then, from far off, like the Voice of Doom, deliberate and awful, came the whispering again:

'THE ST PAUL'S WHICH WE SEE TODAY IS THE THIRD CATHEDRAL WHICH HAS BEEN BUILT *DE NOVO* ON THE SITE IT OCCUPIES. THE FIRST CATHEDRAL OF THE WHISPER WHICH WE HAVE AUTHENTIC RECORD WAS THAT ERECTED BY ETHELBERT, KING OF KENT. SIR CHRISTOPHER WREN, ARCHITECT OF THE PRESENT BUILDING, LIVED TO SEE HIS HANDIWORK COMPLETED, AND DIED IN 1723. AND NOW, LADIES AND GENTLEMEN, IF YOU WILL KINDLY CONTINUE YOUR JOURNEY–'

I rose from my seat.

And at that moment, as distinct and deliberate as the guide's, a man's whisper ran along the wall: 'DARLING, I LOVE YOU!'

Shocked, I prepared to continue my journey. But a worse thing happened. A woman's whisper smote my ear, impersonal, like all whispers, but unmistakably feminine: 'AND I LOVE YOU.'

Then came a male whisper – and now indeed like the Voice of Doom:

'PRIVATE CONVERSATION IS NOT ALLOWED IN THE GALLERY. YOU WILL PLEASE RETURN IMMEDIATELY.'

Shamefaced, we slunk back and met at the entrance, scarce daring to look at each other. Jean, I noticed, had a heightened colour; so had Stephen. Phyllis looked perfectly cool, but her eyes sparkled. Mr Gordon Smith was a bright red. The guide was grim.

'Now, ladies and gentlemen,' he said, barring the way, 'this won't do, you know. A joke's a joke – *outside* the precincts; but this is a thing that's never happened before, to my knowledge, in the whole history of the Cathedral. I'm sorry, but I'm afraid I must ask for an apology, if it's to go no further.'

There was a dead silence – save for a curious muffled sound from Phyllis. From the look of Stephen's face I judged that he was considering the legal aspect of the matter.

'I'm quite sure,' I said, at last, gravely, 'that whoever was responsible will be only too glad to apologize. The question is, Who was it? Or, rather, Who were it? For my part, I was quite unable to identify the voices.'

I looked from face to face; and once again there was a dead silence.

'Well, sir,' said the guide, kindly, 'I can see it's a delicate matter. Perhaps you'd like to go up to the Round Gallery and have it out among yourselves. But I've got to have an explanation before you go,' he finished, firmly.

'Look here, my man,' said Stephen, the lawyer breaking out, 'you've no right to detain us, you know.'

'Really, really, Stephen,' I said, 'you can hardly wish to bring this painful episode into the courts. You, of all people,' I added.

'What do you mean?' said Stephen, fiercely.

'Let us go up to the Round Gallery,' I said.

The Round Gallery is out of doors; and it was full of sun. We looked out over London, and London River and the haze of summer. We looked in silence.

'Well,' I said at last, 'we must face it. As a married man, and the only one of the party against whom there can be no sort of suspicion, perhaps I had better conduct the investigation. Is that agreed?'

'No,' said Stephen.

'As regards the man,' I went on, '(I shall try to mention no names), there is one among us who is notoriously shy and diffident in matters of the heart; and what more natural than that he should have seized this opportunity to declare himself at a distance? On the other hand–'

'If you mean *me*–' said Stephen, hotly.

'I name no names. On the other hand, we have also a bolder one among us, who would be less likely to shrink from so audacious an act as this.'

'If you mean *me*–' began Mr Gordon Smith.

'I name no names. In the former case, the identity of the lady would, of course, be clear enough.' (I glanced at Jean, but both she and Phyllis were gazing at the Thames.) 'In the latter case, it might be one or the other–'

'Really, Mr Moon!' said Phyllis, protesting.

'One or the other,' I repeated.

'I tell you what *I* think–' said Mr Smith, explosively, looking hard at me.

'Yes, Gordon?' said Phyllis, haughtily, looking hard at Mr Smith.

Mr Smith said no more.

'I think, perhaps,' said Phyllis, 'as Mr Moon is a married man, and therefore *quite* above suspicion, the best thing would be for *him* to take the blame – formally – and thus relieve the real culprit from an embarrassing confession.'

'Very well,' I said. 'For the general good – I am ready to do that; provided it is understood to be a purely formal confession, having no relation to the truth. Do you agree, Stephen?'

Stephen grunted a grudging assent.

'You two men,' said Phyllis – 'or one of you – should be grateful to Mr Moon.'

The two men glared gratefully at Mr Moon.

'I don't know about that,' said Mr Smith, sulkily. 'And what about the lady's apology?'

'I think perhaps Jean and I had better toss up,' said Phyllis.

'What for?' said Jean, drowsily.

'Heads, Phyllis,' I called, 'tails, Jean,' and I spun a coin.

'Heads,' said everybody.

'Damn!' said Mr Smith, surprisingly.

'Well,' said Phyllis, brightly, 'I'll do it – for Jean's sake. But it seems a shame. Come, Mr Moon, we'll go and confess.'

'I think, perhaps,' I said, 'the others had better leave us to go through this ordeal alone. It will be less embarrassing.'

Jean departed dreamily down the stairs and Stephen immediately followed. Mr Smith hesitated, but remained.

'Goodness knows,' said Phyllis, 'it will be embarrassing enough, in any case, Mr Moon, to confess to such a thing.'

'But how much more embarrassing it would be,' I said, 'for the guilty parties.'

'True,' said Phyllis. 'As for you, Gordon, I'm surprised at you.'

'It wasn't *me*,' said Mr Smith, warmly. 'You know I wouldn't dream of saying such a thing!'

'Not even to Jean?' said Phyllis.

'Not even to either of you!' said the boy, strangely.

'You're not very polite,' said Phyllis, sighing. 'Then it must have been Stephen. Please leave us, Gordon.'

'How do I know you won't shirk it?' said Mr Smith, stubbornly.

'I shall go through with it, I promise you,' I said. 'But, of course, if you would rather confess yourself–'

Mr Smith departed, muttering. We followed at a distance.

'Anyhow,' I said, 'I feel exceptionally noble.'

'I feel pretty good myself,' said Phyllis.

'I wonder who it was, *really*.'

'I wonder,' said Phyllis.

CHAPTER 4

In The Lift

'I suppose I can trust you,' said Phyllis anxiously, 'with this lift.'

'A man who can be trusted with you,' I answered, proudly, 'can be trusted with anything. And the lift, at least, does what it's told. So.' I pressed the button, and we descended.

We had been dancing at Boom's, a small and (so I am always told) select dancing club, Phyllis, Jean Renton, Mr Gordon Smith, and I; also Stephen Trout and Lettice Trout, his sister, a good woman, but one who craves excitement, and fondly hopes to find it by inducing her brother to take her to the more respectable night clubs.

Boom's is extremely respectable; the only thing to be said against it is that it consistently breaks the law concerned with the consumption of alcoholic refreshment. And so jealous of its reputation is Boom's, that the club has taken special precautions to prevent the entry of His Majesty's police.

This lift is one of the precautions. Except for the fire-escape, the lift is the only avenue of approach to Boom's, which is on the top floor of a high building in Shaftesbury Avenue. There are no stairs. The lift is very small, holding two comfortably, or three at a pinch. It is worked by the members. But at the lower end of the shaft, on the fifth floor, stands the club commissionaire, with instructions to admit almost anybody, but not the police.

We were leaving at the ridiculous hour of 12.30 a.m., for Miss Lettice Trout had early wearied of excitement, and, declaring that the last thing she wished to do was to break up the party, had succeeded in doing that very thing. She, with Mr Gordon Smith, had preceded us in the lift, and Stephen Trout, with Jean Renton, was waiting above to follow us.

I will not pretend that I was in an extremely good temper, for up till that moment I had paid the entire expenses of the party, and, having had one dance with Phyllis, and three with Lettice Trout, I was not entirely satisfied with my investment.

'This is rather a shame,' I said, mildly. 'To go to bed at the puritanical hour of 12.30, after exactly five dances (three with Lettice Trout), and you in a new dress–'

Phyllis had a new dress – a new dress, which I cannot describe; but it was silver and simple, and artfully artless, like Phyllis.

'I know,' said Phyllis, with what she fondly thinks is a pout, but is, in fact, only a most admirable arrangement of her mouth and a most attractive trick with her nose. 'It was hardly worth while putting it on.'

'It was very well worth while,' I said, warmly; and in the circumstances, and the light in the lift being bright, I can hardly be blamed if I turned to get the full effect of Phyllis and the new dress before the lift stopped.

And at that moment the lift did stop.

On three sides of us was looking-glass. On the fourth was a blank wall, painted an unpleasant shade of green.

'Oo!' said Phyllis. 'Whatever's happened?'

'It's stopped,' I said, intelligently, playing with the buttons.

'I noticed that,' said Phyllis. 'But why?'

'Why not?' I said.

'There are several good answers to that question,' said she; 'but would you mind doing something first, Mr Moon?'

I feverishly pressed the same buttons in a different order. Nothing happened.

'It's no good,' I said. 'We're stuck.'

All was silent. We were alone in space.

'I'm frightened,' said Phyllis; and then, surprisingly, 'Oh, John, what fun!'

'Yes,' I said, reflectively, pressing the same buttons again.

'What *will* mother say?' said Phyllis. 'I think perhaps you'd better do something, Mr Moon.'

'I will, I will,' I said; and all the responsibility of manhood rose up in me. I pressed the buttons again, with the same result.

'I was once stuck in a Tube lift,' I said wisely. 'They brought up another lift alongside, and we escaped through a door in the side of the lift.'

'But there is no other lift here,' said Phyllis.

'True. And there is no door.'

'Have you any other plans of that kind?' said Phyllis, after a slight pause.

'I know what I shall do. I shall call down to Lettice Trout. I feel that in some way she is responsible for this. Hullo!' I called, my voice echoing hollow in the shaft. 'Hullo there! Miss Trout! Gordon! Lettice Trout!' And then, quite simply, 'Lettice?'

'Hullo!' came up a faint, thin voice. 'Come on, Mr Moon! We're waiting.'

'So are we,' I returned.

'Why don't you come down?' called Mr

Smith, impatiently. (I am not at all sure that Mr Smith and Lettice will ever marry.)

'We can't.'

'What? I can't hear.'

At this point a loud voice fell on us from above – Stephen Trout's.

'Why don't you send up the lift?' said he.

'We can't.'

'What's that? I can't hear. Where are you?'

'THE FACT OF THE MATTER IS,' I shouted, 'WE ARE NEITHER HERE NOR THERE. THE LIFT HAS STOPPED.'

'WHAT?'

'I SAY – THE – LIFT – HAS – STOPPED.'

'WHERE?'

'HERE.'

Two voices said simultaneously, a long way off, 'He says the lift has stopped,' and one could almost hear the busy brains clicking below and above.

The next voice was the commissionaire's, an ex-sergeant, a practical man.

'HULLO, SIR!' he cried. 'CAN'T YOU BUDGE HER?'

'I AM QUITE UNABLE TO BUDGE HER.'

'I NEVER KNEW IT TO HAPPEN BEFORE, SIR,' he shouted.

'THAT'S VERY COMFORTING.'

'BEG PARDON, SIR?'

'I SAY – IT'S VERY COMFORTING.'

'TRY PRESSING THE BUTTON,' called Mr Smith, helpfully.

'I'VE TRIED THAT. I THOUGHT OF THAT ALMOST IMMEDIATELY.'

'TRY SHIFTING YOUR WEIGHT, SIR,' put in the commissionaire.

'VERY WELL,' I yelled, moving a little closer to Phyllis, and I pressed the buttons again.

'DOESN'T THAT HELP?' called Mr Smith.

'IT'S A PLEASANT CHANGE,' I replied; 'BUT IT SEEMS TO MAKE NO DIFFERENCE. WHAT SHALL I TRY NOW?'

There was silence.

Then the voice of Lettice came up: 'DON'T BE FRIGHTENED, PHYLLIS! WE'LL WAIT FOR YOU.'

'IT'S ALL RIGHT,' cried Phyllis, powdering her nose. 'I'M NOT FRIGHTENED. BUT IT'S NICE TO KNOW YOU'RE THERE.'

'*What?*'

'I SAY – IT'S NICE – TO – KNOW – YOU'RE THERE.'

'And not here,' I added, softly.

'That wasn't what I meant, Mr Moon,' said Phyllis.

'Of course.'

'THE COMMISSIONAIRE,' came from Mr Smith, 'HAS GONE FOR AN ELECTRICIAN.

HE WON'T BE LONG.'

'DON'T BE FRIGHTENED, PHYLLIS,' cried Jean.

'WE'LL WAIT,' cried Lettice, nobly, 'IF IT'S ALL NIGHT.'

'I HOPE IT WON'T BE THAT,' I yelled. 'MEANWHILE, THIS GENERAL CONVERSATION IS BECOMING RATHER A STRAIN, SO YOU WON'T THINK US RUDE, I HOPE, IF WE DON'T TALK VERY MUCH.'

'*What?*' cried Mr Smith.

'I SAID – THIS CONVERSATION MUST NOW CEASE,' I croaked; 'MY VOICE IS GOING.'

There was silence, but for muffled murmurs, above and below. We hung suspended, like souls in the blue, listening to the remote and unimportant voices of Earth and Heaven at once.

'Well, I'm going to sit down,' said Phyllis, doing so.

'And I.'

'I'm not sure that you hadn't better stand, Mr Moon.'

'I'm quite sure I hadn't,' I said, sitting down.

'Something might happen,' said Phyllis, making room for me, 'and you won't be ready.'

'I shall be quite ready. Besides, I must keep up my strength for the next emergency. And this is an opportunity, as Mr Joseph Chamberlain remarked, which may never occur again.'

'This is rather an adventure, John,' said Phyllis. 'Do you think we are in any danger?'

'At any moment the electrician may arrive.'

'Oh! is that all? You don't think the lift may suddenly drop to the basement?' said Phyllis, hopefully.

'No,' I said, 'it won't do that. But if there was an earthquake, there is no doubt we should be in a tight place.'

'What a terrible thought, Mr Moon! But so would Jean and Stephen.'

'True,' I said. 'I like to think of Jean and Stephen sitting up there. They say that there is nothing like a common danger for drawing people together, Phyllis.'

'Do they say that John? You mean that our danger may be the means of drawing Jean and Stephen together, Mr Moon?'

'Perhaps,' I said. 'Then, of course, there are the other two. I like to think of them.'

'I'm afraid it will take more than an earthquake to draw Lettice and Gordon together,' said Phyllis. 'You ought to be very sorry for Gordon, Mr Moon.'

'Not very,' I said. 'He is being educated – and this is one of his lessons.'

'What is he learning, Mr Moon?'

'The value of a certain lady.'

'Miss Lettice Trout?'

'No,' I said, 'I wasn't thinking of her. He questioned once,' I went on, 'whether the lady had much *in* her. Compared with Jean, for example.'

'The little beast!' said Phyllis. 'Not that it matters to me,' she added, hastily.

'Well, well, he's learning,' I said, tolerantly.

Phyllis nestled back in her corner.

'What shall we talk about now, John?' she said, after a slight pause. 'This is a very comfy little lift, I must say.'

'The decorations are very curious,' I said. 'Have you ever seen a lift with a roof like that before?'

'I don't remember looking at the roof of a lift before. What's the matter with it?'

'It is covered with some sort of berry.'

'So it is,' said Phyllis. 'Grapes.'

'It looks to me,' I said, 'like mistletoe.'

'Grapes, I think, Mr Moon.'

'Mistletoe, Miss Fair.'

'ARE YOU ALL RIGHT, PHYLLIS?' cried Lettice, suddenly, below.

'YES, THANK YOU,' sang Phyllis – 'AT LEAST, I THINK SO.'

'Why the doubt?'

'Those berries are grapes, Mr Moon,' said Phyllis, firmly, looking at me.

'Why?' said I, looking at Phyllis.

'Because I *will* have it so.'

'Very well,' I said.

'I'M ALL RIGHT, LETTICE,' she sang again. 'DON'T WORRY! HOW'S GORDON?'

'I'M ALL RIGHT,' said Mr Smith, grimly.

'HE'S NOT BEHAVING VERY NICELY,' piped Lettice.

'OH, DEAR!' said Phyllis, 'I'M SURPRISED AT THAT. MR MOON'S BEHAVING BEAUTIFULLY.'

Then she leaned back her head against the corner so that I saw three lovely necks instead of one, closed her eyes, and said, 'What shall we talk about now, John?'

'A little devil,' I said, sighing.

'I beg your pardon?'

The strains of dance music came faintly from above. 'It's curious,' I said, 'by what illogical rules our lives are governed–'

'Oh, dear!' said Phyllis. 'I know that beginning. It generally ends in something bad.'

'Only half an hour ago,' I said, 'I held you closely in my arms before a crowd of people,

68

and we moved several times round the room in a prolonged and intimate embrace. We might have been married–'

'We very nearly were, you know.'

'Do not let us open old wounds, Miss Fair. The present are enough. All this, as I say, was done in public, and no man thought the worse of us–'

'With the possible exception of Mr Smith,' said Phyllis.

'With the possible exception of Mr Smith,' I agreed. 'But his objection (if any) was in no sense a moral one – quite the contrary – being, in fact, if you are right, a selfish regret that he was not doing as I was doing.'

'He was – with Lettice.'

'Quite. An entirely proper proceeding. Yet here, where no mortal eye can see us, if I were so much as to put an arm about you, a strong objection would be taken–'

'It would,' said Phyllis.

'Assuming, that is, that there was anyone to see – which there is not.'

'I don't think that makes any difference,' said Phyllis.

'My point exactly. When other people are there they make no difference at all – as we saw upstairs. Logically, therefore, a *fortiori*–'

'*A* what?'

'*A fortiori* – they must make still less difference when they are not there – as here–'

'Are you sure you're still being logical, Mr Moon?' said Phyllis, doubtfully.

'Perfectly. I have proved that it cannot be wrong to do in private that which may be done without reproach in public.'

'I suppose you have, John,' said Phyllis, settling herself comfortably again. 'All the same, I don't think we'd better have any more logic, Mr Moon.'

'ARE YOU ALL RIGHT, LETTICE, DEAR?'

'YES, DEAR.'

'THIS *IS* A COMFY LIFT.'

'WE'RE SITTING ON THE STAIRS,' said Mr Smith.

'THERE'S A DRAUGHT,' said Lettice.

'SEVERAL DRAUGHTS,' said Mr Smith.

'OH, DEAR!' said Phyllis. 'I *AM* SORRY. WE'RE *QUITE* COSY.'

There was a distant grunting sound.

'The question of the berries,' I continued, ignoring these interruptions, 'is not a question of logic, but of fact.'

'I'm very glad of that, Mr Moon.'

'But here, again, logic has something to say.'

'Oh, dear!'

'It is absurd,' I said, 'how much importance is attached in literature and drama, and indeed in life, to that form of personal salute which we call a kiss. Why, for example, should it so often be regarded as a wrongful act, and, on the stage, be generally the turning point in several lives? After all, what *is* a kiss?'

'I haven't the least idea, Mr Moon.'

'A kiss is the most beautiful and romantic fashion of greeting known to mankind. Thus the loyal subject salutes his king, thus mothers their children, thus sister signifies her love for sister. And most innocent of all, perhaps most hallowed by tradition, is the sportive kiss which is given under the mistletoe.'

'I thought we agreed they were grapes, Mr Moon.'

'It is at once a courtesy,' I went on 'and the formal expression of a spiritual bond, like a handshake. Like a handshake, it may be sincerely intended or not; but in either case it does no harm – no one is the wiser – and no one is the worse.'

'In fact, Mr Moon – if I understand you aright – properly considered, a kiss is no more than a "How d'ye do?" or a friendly word in a letter.'

'You mustn't be frivolous, Miss Fair. As I

was saying, we are very old friends, and if I were to signify my esteem for you by warmly shaking you by the hand – so – no one would have a word to say. By the same reasoning, I can see no sort of harm in my expressing the same sentiments in the other, and the more historic, manner.'

'But even a handshake, Mr Moon, may be prolonged beyond the limits of decorum.'

'I was not speaking of *long* handshakes, Miss Fair.'

'I'm glad of that, John,' said Phyllis. 'In that case – perhaps–'

'CHEER UP,' shouted Mr Smith. 'THE ELECTRICIAN'S ARRIVED.'

Neither Phyllis nor I uttered any immediate expression of satisfaction.

'GOOD!' I shouted, in a moment or two.

'Well, well,' said Phyllis, sighing. 'I shall be quite sorry to leave our little lift. Though I must say you've talked a great deal of nonsense in it.'

'You were wrong about the berries, you know.'

'I suppose I was,' said Phyllis. 'Otherwise, of course, you would never have behaved as you have, would you, Mr Moon?'

'Certainly not,' I said.

'I don't agree with anything else you've

said, Mr Moon. You understand that?'

'Perfectly.'

Mr Smith's voice was heard.

'THE ELECTRICIAN SAYS HE CAN'T DO NOTHING.'

Then there was silence.

Then: 'HE SAYS, TRY SHIFTING YOUR WEIGHT AGAIN, AND IF THAT DON'T DO IT HE'LL HAVE TO CLIMB DOWN AND BREAK THROUGH THE ROOF.'

'Oh, dear!' said Phyllis, with a faint scream, 'and spoil the mistletoe.'

'RIGHT!' I returned, and I prepared to attack the buttons again.

'I've noticed one thing, Mr Moon,' said Phyllis.

'What's that?'

'There's one button you haven't pressed at all, Mr Moon,' said Phyllis, gravely.

'Ah!' I said, 'you noticed that, did you? Perhaps we'd better try it now.'

'Perhaps we'd better.'

Miraculously the lift descended, to the sound of cheers.

'Why didn't you press that button yourself, Miss Fair?' I said.

'I thought you knew best, Mr Moon,' said Phyllis. 'Hullo, Gordon! I hope you've been behaving.'

CHAPTER 5

A Quiet Sunday Morning

Phyllis rang me up in bed. It was Sunday morning, early – well, early for Sunday morning. That is to say, I had begun my second sausage and poured out my second cup of tea, and the bells for matins were not yet audible; also I had read through the first four columns of Mr Garvin, and had decided not to go to church, after all; for, if Mr Garvin is in form, enough is as good as a priest.

I was also thinking, in between the lines, in a maudlin sort of way, of my wife and home; for with the best sausages in the world, and Mr Garvin at the top of his form, a club bedroom on a Sunday morning is not exhilarating. I had even indulged in a few sad, sentimental thoughts about my garden; I had even wondered if my dear wife Angela was doing the same. It is part of our agreement that such thoughts must be instantly suppressed; for they are the beginning of the end. On the first occasion that we agreed to separate judiciously for a month these thoughts occurred to both of us at the end of the first week; recklessly we both returned home and were reunited, quarrelled violently the following day, and had to separate again. Today the statutory month had still some time to run; I suppressed my thoughts and murmured a line or two to Liberty and Independence.

I was therefore definitely agreeable to hear Phyllis Fair's voice. Phyllis is one of those rare creatures whose pleasing voice invariably survives the telephone. I know many a sweet, distinguished voice; but the Post Office reduces nearly all of them to the deadly level of an early gramophone. Phyllis alone is defiantly Phyllis and no other. Nor is she one of those bright-voiced gay telephone talkers. The voice is never raised. But far away there is a soft and vital murmur, electric, comforting, and thrilling all at once, like a violet ray. I don't know how she does it. She says herself the secret is to be found on Page 1 of the Directions: 'PLACE THE LIPS AS CLOSE AS POSSIBLE TO THE TRANSMITTER MOUTHPIECE.' But I do not think it is as simple as that.

'Good morning, John,' said Phyllis. 'Are

you doing anything this morning?'

'I have still a column of Mr Garvin to read,' I said. 'For the rest, my day is free. I could call quite soon.'

'Don't be so hasty,' said Phyllis. 'I'm having my portrait painted. At Mary Banbury's. And I thought perhaps you'd care to come and watch.'

'That depends. Am I to watch the painting or the painted?'

'The painters, John. There are three of them. All ladies, Mr Moon. And they *will* talk scandal all the time. So I want you to be there.'

'Thank you very much. But I should hate to be a killjoy. Why shouldn't they talk scandal? Perhaps it's the only thing they know.'

'I don't want them to talk at all. They don't get on with it. And it doesn't suit the picture.'

'I don't follow.'

'How very dense of you! The picture's to be called "Miss Innocence," Mr Moon. What did you say, Mr Moon?'

'I was clearing my throat,' I said. 'I see. And if they talk scandal, it makes you look scandalous?'

'*They* make me look scandalous,' corrected Phyllis.

'It's the same thing,' I said.

'It isn't at all. Perhaps, after all, you'd better not come, Mr Moon.'

'I'll be round in half an hour,' I said. 'By the way, why are you having *three* portraits done?'

'It's a competition. The one that wins is to be sent in for the "Beauty Toilet Soap Poster Competition." The second best is to be offered to the *Green Magazine* for a cover. The other will be sent to the Royal Academy. I'm to be the judge.'

'*I* shall be the judge,' I said; 'for I am perhaps the best living authority. Goodbye.'

A few minutes later Mrs Banbury rang up. Mrs Banbury is the kind of woman who generally contrives to ring up a gentleman when the whole of his face and a great part of his hands are thickly covered with shaving soap. Today she hit it off to a second.

I seized – and soaped – the receiver.

'Yes?' I said, soaping slightly the transmitter mouthpiece.

A wild, bright, energetic voice assaulted me, not pausing for breath: 'That Robin Moon? Mary Banbury speaking, look here, you doing anything this morning? Lettice Trout, Jean Renton, and I are painting

Phyllis Fair, why don't you come along and have a quiet morning in the studio?'

'Why should I?' I asked, with an effect of reluctance.

'Well, the fact is, we don't seem to be getting *on*. You see, she *will* talk the whole time—'

'Extraordinary,' I murmured, smiling through my soap. 'What does she talk about?'

'Scandal, chiefly. And, of course, that makes the rest of us talk. And we don't get on.'

'But, surely, if *you* didn't talk *she* wouldn't talk. From what I know of Miss Fair she'd hate talking to herself.'

'I know,' said Mrs Banbury, with a certain inconsistence. 'We've tried that. But if nobody talks her face goes all dead, and she generally goes to sleep. What I thought was that if you were there you might be able to keep her interested without making her talk, d'you see?'

'What made you think that, Mrs Banbury?' I asked, wonderingly.

'I dunno,' said Mrs Banbury.

'Am I to juggle?' I said, 'or do card-tricks, or what?'

'Oh, no! just talk; but in a general sort of way. Do come. Besides,' she added, a little grimly, 'I want to have a talk with you, Mr Moon.'

'Not scandal, I hope?'

'I'm not so sure,' she answered, darkly.

'Well, well, I'll see if I can manage it,' I said.

I washed down the telephone, and shaved reflectively. I am very much afraid that Mrs Banbury does not extravagantly *like* me; and I for one don't blame her. But what amazes me is that she should not approve of me. For though I am fully as respectable as she (in many ways more so), I know that if she was ever assured of this she would be deeply disappointed. It is only the suspicion that I and many other of our mutual friends are not wholly respectable that keeps Mrs Banbury alive. All night this Earth of ours labours painfully round the Sun, and at the last the day breaks, a golden splendour in the east, with no other purpose than to give Mrs Banbury another opportunity to discuss those suspicions and hand them on to such (if any) as know not of them. Then why – But there, of what use is Reason in these affairs?

Poor Jack Banbury. A very docile fellow. All the same, I can't help *liking* Mrs Banbury.

I found in her studio a model throne, three business-like easels arranged *en échelon* and four ladies on a divan, smoking cigarettes – and talking.

'Business as usual,' I remarked, brightly.

'Late, as usual,' said Mrs Banbury.

'Good morning, Miss Fair,' I said, and I went on hastily, and rashly, 'you'll forgive this intrusion, I hope? Entirely Mary's fault.'

Phyllis made a small face at me, and Mrs Banbury said drily, 'Intrusion? Phyllis says she asked you too.'

'True,' I said, floundering slightly; 'but it was you who persuaded me.'

And I glanced gallantly at Mrs Banbury, and deprecatingly at Phyllis – a very difficult thing to do. The first half of the operation was the more successful, I fancied.

'Come along,' said Mrs Banbury. 'I'm dying to paint.'

'So am I,' said Jean Renton, with her own particular languor, not as if she was dying to do anything but rather as if she would do anything to die.

There now took place a great deal of arrangement. Phyllis was arranged on the throne, and the artists severally arranged their easels and their chairs, and they all held up their fingers and squinted at Phyllis, and pushed their chairs back an inch or two, squinted again and replaced the chairs. When all was ready Mrs Banbury pulled down the blind and they began again. Then they pulled up the blind and rearranged Phyllis. I sat unobtrusively in the window behind the artists, and it so happened that if I chanced to turn my eyes towards the throne and Phyllis chanced to turn her eyes towards the window, our eyes might quite conceivably meet.

'Now Mr Moon's to do the talking,' said Mrs Banbury at last, 'and nobody's to answer him – especially not the model.'

'This, indeed, is a rare opportunity,' I said.

'But you must talk about something *interesting,* y'know – to keep the model lively. Don't you feel the draught there, Mr Moon?'

'He doesn't *look* cold,' said the model, glancing at the window.

'This way, please, Phyllis,' said Lettice Trout, severely. 'I'm doing your eyes.'

They painted in absolute silence for two minutes. I gave them a brief outline of the political situation. The model sat like a statue, looking innocent to the verge of dullness. She was dressed in a pink flounced dancing-frock, with a fan upon her lap.

'You're not looking a bit lively, Phyllis,' said Mrs Banbury, squinting at her. 'I saw your wife the other day, Mr Moon,' she went on, inconsequently.

'Oh!' I said. 'Is she in town?'

'Dancing. At Boom's. With Major Trevor.'

'A very gallant officer,' I said.

'I call it indecent,' said Mrs Banbury, 'the way you two go on.'

'The way we go off, you mean? It would be more decent, I suppose, if we separated altogether?'

'It would give Mary more to talk about,' said the model.

'On the contrary,' I said, 'the topic would be exhausted in a week. But, as things are, our marriage is likely to go on forever. And Mr and Mrs Banbury will never lack a subject for conversation.'

They painted in silence for a few moments – Lettice Trout with business concentration, Jean rapt and her eyes half closed, Mrs Banbury with much sitting back and gasping and sighing and waving her brush and putting her head on one side.

'I hear you were stuck in a lift, you and Phyllis,' she remarked casually, after one of these pauses.

'Yes,' I said. 'I seem to remember something of the sort.'

'It must have been a great bore.'

'It was,' I said, glancing at the model.

'Don't move, please, Phyllis,' said Lettice Trout.

'I didn't move,' said the model.

'Your eyes moved.'

'And how long were you in the lift, Mr Moon?' said Mrs Banbury, poising a brush, like a man about to harpoon a whale.

'Five minutes – ten. What period would you say, Phyllis?'

'I mustn't say anything,' said the model.

'It was half an hour,' said Lettice Trout, grimly, having waited down below.

'You poor dears,' sighed Mrs Banbury, with an appearance of compassion. 'What *did* you do with yourselves?'

'What *can* one do in a lift?' I said. 'We just talked.'

'You're looking much livelier now, Phyllis,' said Mrs Banbury.

'But not a bit innocent,' said Lettice Trout.

The model looked exceedingly roguish and adorable, but said nothing. There was half a minute's hard painting.

'What did you talk about in the lift?' said

the insatiable Mrs Banbury at last.

'About poor Jean and Stephen Trout, chiefly,' I said, with a certain low cunning. 'They were waiting up above, you know.'

'*I* rather enjoyed it,' said Jean, suddenly breaking silence, and blushing all over.

Mrs Banbury was off at once after the new hare. 'Jean! How thrilling! Did he propose? Do tell us. What did he say?'

'He talked about law-cases.'

'That means he's feeling sentimental,' remarked the model, with authority.

'Be quiet, Phyllis,' said Mrs B.

'She's quite right,' I remarked. 'Most men when profoundly moved start talking about their work; all barristers do.'

'I wish you'd all be quiet,' said Mrs B, with a lingering pretence of interest in her canvas. 'I've messed up the mouth. What do you mean by law-cases, Jean?'

'All sorts of cases. There was one Chancery, and one a contract, I think he said, and one about a Belgian tobacco manufacturer. And he was just beginning on a divorce case, when–'

'That means he's going to propose!' exclaimed the model delightedly, clapping her hands.

'SIT STILL, Phyllis!' cried the exasperated

artists. And 'Is this *your* story, or Jean's?' said Mrs B warmly – and unwisely.

'It *was* my story,' said Phyllis, demurely, but unpardonably, 'and I hope it's going to be Jean's.'

It was now Lettice Trout's turn to fly the red flag.

'No one was surprised when you threw Stephen over,' she said, hotly; 'but you might at least have the decency to keep quiet about it.'

'Oh, I don't mind,' said Jean, kindly soul.

'Well, I do,' said Lettice, 'and I'm quite sure my brother would never propose to two women in the same way. Sit still, please; I'm doing that eye.'

'I thought you'd done that eye,' said the model.

'I see it very differently now,' said Lettice, viciously mixing a horrible greenish mess on her palette.

'If you think I'm going to sit here–' began Phyllis, with spirit.

'*Quiet, quiet!*' wailed Mrs B. 'Now then, not another word.'

There was silence.

'Well, Jean,' she said, almost immediately, 'and what happened?'

'Nothing,' said Jean, dreamily. 'Just then

the lift started, and we went home.'

'What would you have said, Jean?' asked Mrs Banbury softly (the curiosity of that woman!).

'I adore him,' said Jean, simply, and we all gasped. Never in the memory of any of us had Jean been known to express a positive preference for any particular man, person, or thing. 'Adore!' It was a miracle.

In sheer stupefaction all remained silent for a minute or two.

'What a shame!' said Mrs B at last. 'Quite a pity the lift started when it did, wasn't it, Mr Moon?'

'It was,' I said.

'Keep still, Phyllis. It started suddenly, didn't it?'

'Very suddenly,' said Lettice Trout.

'Lifts do start suddenly,' I said.

'It was almost a pity you and Phyllis didn't know, Mr Moon,' said Mrs B.

'Know what, Mrs Banbury?'

'That Stephen was just going to propose to Jean.'

'It would have been nice to know, of course,' I said; 'but how would that have helped?'

'You and Phyllis might have stayed in the lift a little longer – for Jean's sake.'

'How could we?' said the model, incautiously. 'The man was just going to break in the roof, anyhow.'

'Oh!' said Mrs B, with a smile I didn't quite like (she should have gone to the Bar). 'So that was it?'

'That was what, Mrs Banbury?' I inquired.

'What did your mother say about it, Phyllis?' she went on, ignoring me.

'She didn't say anything about it,' said the model. 'Neither did I,' she added.

'I was thinking of calling on your mother one day this week,' said Mrs Banbury. 'Will she be at home, Phyllis?'

'Not this week' said the model, shortly.

'Not Thursday, Phyllis?'

'Not any day.'

After that there was the longest silence of the morning. The artists worked feverishly. I strolled round behind them, and studied Mrs Banbury's production.

'It's quite *like*, I think,' she said, dubiously; 'but it's such a terrible *drawing*. It's turned out quite different today.'

'I don't think mine's very *like*,' said Lettice; 'but it's quite a good drawing, don't you think?'

Jean said nothing.

None of my artist friends has ever yet produced a picture which was at the same time 'like', and a good drawing. It is very strange.

'What exactly is the point of a portrait which is a good drawing but not "like"?' I inquired.

'Economic use of the materials,' said Lettice, 'for one thing. Good, clean line. And getting *inside* the model. Just what the artist *sees* in her. As simply as possible. The *essentials*. After all, you don't want a *photograph, do* you?'

'It depends,' I said, doubtfully, examining the portrait. 'Is that what you see in the sitter, Lettice?'

'Yes. Another artist, of course, may see something quite different.'

'I hope so,' I murmured, passing behind Mrs B.

'I hope so,' I murmured again, passing behind Jean.

'What do they see in me, Mr Moon?' said the model, demurely.

'Mrs Banbury – a cat,' I said, 'green-eyed, dangerous, conscienceless, voracious. Miss Trout – a kitten, green-eyed, playful, seductive, heartless. And Miss Renton – God bless her! – a canary, a little canary, frightened, innocent, a thing of joy, in a kind of cage.'

'A lift, perhaps,' said Mrs Banbury.

'*Well,*' said the model, jumping to her feet, 'I think, perhaps, I'd better go home.'

'The truth, of course–' I began.

'YES, MR MOON?' said four eager voices in unison.

'Is stranger than the pictures. Goodbye, Mrs Banbury. I hope I've been a help.'

'You have, indeed. I feel we've got at the real Phyllis this morning.'

'Cat, kitten, or canary?' said Phyllis.

'All three,' said Mrs Banbury. 'Mr Moon is right. We're wasting our time. The real Phyllis will never be discovered. Not in a picture.'

'There are always the movies,' said Lettice Trout, unkindly.

'On the contrary,' said I, 'the real Phyllis (I hope) will shortly be discovered in the Park – with me.'

'I believe she will,' said Phyllis. 'And a pleasant change it will be, Mr Moon.'

'I shall certainly call on your mother,' said Mrs Banbury.

CHAPTER 6

Birds Of A Feather

'I asked you to call today,' said Phyllis, 'because Mary Banbury is coming.'

'A very poor reason,' I said. 'I don't want to see Mary Banbury.'

'She doesn't want to see you,' said Phyllis. 'You know what she's coming for?'

'Not precisely. But, in general, when Mary Banbury moves from one place to another she has one of two purposes – either to collect information or to distribute it.'

'Exactly. She's going to tell tales. And I thought,' said Phyllis, 'you might perhaps be able to take the wind out of her tales.'

'That would be too cruel,' I said, 'for then there would be nothing left of them.'

'You're very bright today, John,' said Phyllis, twinkling. 'That's lucky – mother doesn't like her,' she went on, playing with those absurd little ribbons she wears in front.

'Your mother has taste.'

'And Mary doesn't like *me*.'

'She has none. But you wrong her. She is merely jealous.'

'Jealous, Mr Moon? Do you mean that she likes *you*? You never told me–'

'Certainly not. Though it is true she follows me about as if she did. "Envious" perhaps is the right word.'

'But why?'

'Because we have adventures, and do odd things, and don't care what people say about them. Because we are desperately wicked–'

'Mr Moon!'

'Or so she supposes. And it is the dream of her life to have adventures and be desperately wicked; but she doesn't dare. Kensington is full of such people; so is Streatham. Streatham finds romance in the imaginary wickedness of film actors. Mary finds romance in the imaginary wickedness of her friends – especially me,' I added. 'I do her a world of good.'

Phyllis twinkled again.

'I think I do my share,' she said, modestly.

'And yet, to do her justice, she also wants to do me good. In fact, if you asked her, she would tell you that her only purpose is to *make* me good. A reformer. She has a mission.'

'She has thick ankles,' said Phyllis, un-kindly.

Just then dear old placid Mrs Fair came in and raised her hands in mock consternation.

'What, you two alone?' she said, subsiding into a large chair. 'What *would* the dear Banbury say. Oh, dear, Mr Moon, I've been hearing such *dreadful* things about you. On the telephone too,' she added, beaming. 'And I do hate scandal on the telephone.'

'I'm sorry,' I said. 'I'm afraid I'm a fraud.'

'Don't tell me that, Mr Moon,' said Mrs Fair, sitting up. 'You're the only young man I believe in, though you do tell such stories.'

'I only meant,' I said, 'that I don't live down to my reputation.'

'Please don't be clever, Mr Moon. Not till I've had a cup of tea. Well, what's this about you and Phyllis being stuck for half an hour in a lift? Goodness, what a place to choose! You might have been killed!'

'I felt quite safe, mother,' said Phyllis. 'One is always safer with a married man.'

'Very true, my dear. But if you want to talk quietly to a married man why don't you take him to a night club, or somewhere sensible! A lift, indeed!'

'We'd just been to a night club,' I put in.

'The lift was more exciting.'

'Then there was something about the Whispering Gallery,' said Mrs Fair. 'Oh, Lord, here she is!'

Mary Banbury was announced and entered, followed rapidly by tea.

Mrs Banbury did *not* sing a hymn of praise at the sight of me.

Mrs Banbury, who, to be fair, is quite good-looking, and dresses assiduously, cocked her little head on one side, and said, 'I didn't expect to see *you* here, Mr Moon.'

'I expect to see *you*,' I said, bowing gracefully, 'wherever I go. Today, however, I came here with a different purpose.'

'I don't doubt you did,' said Mrs Banbury, grimly, turning to Phyllis. But Phyllis only chuckled at her. I wish she would take Mrs Banbury seriously. It is so much more amusing.

Mrs Banbury sat down, took a cup of tea, and destroyed three people's reputations in five words. Then, 'Dear Mrs Fair,' she said, handing up her cup, 'I want to have a quiet talk with you afterwards.'

'Oh, dear!' said the old lady, puffing, 'I know what that means. Can't you tell Phyllis, Mary? She arranges all my gossip for me.'

'No,' said Mrs Banbury. 'This is worse than gossip.'

'There is only one thing worse than gossip,' said Phyllis, with innocent, wide-open eyes. 'And that is the truth. You're not going to begin *that*, Mary?'

'Goodness, child, what dreadful things you say!' said her mother, beaming with pleasure.

'Gossip,' said Mrs Banbury, her eyes bright for battle, 'concerns the past. I am concerned with the future; which may' – and her voice fell hollow, and her eye fell on me – 'which may be worse.'

'If it's Mr Moon you mean,' said Mrs Fair, comfortably, 'I'm sure nothing could be worse than *his* past, judging from what you've told me about it, Mary – at various times.'

Mrs Banbury hurriedly set down her cup, and came as near choking as it is possible for a lady to do at afternoon tea.

To cover her confusion I rose, placed my back to the fender, and cleared my throat, as one about to make an important pronouncement.

'Mrs Fair,' I said, 'I shall shortly leave you to your quiet talk with Mrs Banbury. But before I go I have something to say to you, which I think Mrs Banbury has a right to hear; and knowing her to be the soul of discretion–'

'Goodness!' said Mrs Fair, fanning herself, 'what's come over the man?'

'It is a confession,' I went on, weakly avoiding her gaze. 'I have recently, on two occasions, been guilty of indiscreet conduct towards your daughter. First, when viewing the Whispering Gallery with a party, which included Miss Fair and another lady, I whispered into the wall the words "I love you"; and though they were both some fifty yards away there is no doubt that the words must be taken to have been addressed – and were so taken – to one or other of the ladies. I cannot defend this action,' I said, glancing at Mrs Banbury, and from her to Phyllis.

'Second,' I went on, after a slight pause to cover my emotion, 'when in a lift with your daughter, in order to enjoy a private and uninterrupted conversation with her, I deliberately pressed the "Stop" button halfway between two floors, and for a period variously estimated as between ten minutes and three-quarters of an hour pretended falsely that the lift had broken down.

'This action also was indefensible,' I continued, half choking. 'Further, as Mrs Banbury has said, the future may be worse; and, rather than run the risk of doing worse, I am now resolved to say goodbye to your daughter forever. Forever,' I repeated brokenly.

Phyllis, much overcome, had buried her face in the end of the sofa. Mrs Banbury was extremely red; but she looked expectantly at Mrs Fair.

That lady opened her mouth and uttered a musical and prolonged peal of laughter.

'Goodness, Mr Moon!' said she, wiping her eyes, 'what nonsense you talk! I thought you were serious for once.'

'Goodbye, Phyllis,' I said, holding out my hand. 'For the last time.'

'Stuff and nonsense!' said Mrs Fair. 'You'll do nothing of the sort. Who's going to take my daughter out, I'd like to know, if the married men desert her?'

'Really, Mrs Fair!' said Mrs Banbury, 'I *must* say–'

'Well, you can't trust the single ones,' said Mrs Fair. 'That I *do* know. They keep her up all hours, they tell her horrible stories, they give her horrible drinks, and as like as not they're after her money, or are only hard up for a dancing-partner. But if a married man bothers to take her out, I do know she'll be treated with proper respect, *and* properly looked after. *And* not worried to death with proposals,' she added.

'You're very trustful,' began Mrs Banbury, a little nastily.

'If I can't trust Phyllis to take care of herself she's no daughter of mine.'

'She is very much a daughter of yours,' I put in, gently.

'All the same,' said the old lady, 'you're not to make her look ridiculous, Mr Moon. And I don't think you ought to make love to any girl in the Whispering Gallery. It's not decent. Take her to a night club, as I said before. And now, dear children, I am going to sleep.'

With which words the old lady closed her eyes and instantly began to snore.

I looked at Mrs Banbury, and Mrs Banbury looked at me. Mrs Banbury opened her mouth, and shut it again, without saying a word. I have never seen this happen before – or since.

'Goodbye,' I said. 'Won't you join us at Boom's one night? We have a party there most Fridays?'

'Jack doesn't dance,' she said, with a strange meekness, eyeing me uncertainly.

'Young Gordon Smith dances very well,' I said, casually.

Mrs Banbury said nothing; but a kind of warm gleam came into her pale-blue eyes, and for the first time she smiled a sort of soft human smile. And for the first time I felt a little wicked.

A few evenings later, acting on Mrs Fair's advice, I was talking to Phyllis in the sitting-out-room at Boom's. Decorations – fantastic; cypresses and deserts. Divans – spacious. Cushions – huge and gay. Lights – shaded and low.

'I have noticed,' I was saying, 'that in haunts of pleasure of this kind it is considered necessary to talk in the manner of the decorations – staccato, smart, unnatural, highly coloured, and rather fatiguing. I'm afraid I can't do it, Phyllis.'

'Please don't try,' said Phyllis. 'I much prefer an ordinary dull man. Listen.'

Close behind sat a couple with their backs to us, talking brightly in the manner described.

'What about another?' said the man.

'Had another – had enough,' was the answer.

'Can't have enough of a good thing.'

'You know too much,' said the woman, with a hard, gay laugh.

'Then shall we circulate?' said the man (meaning 'dance').

'I think I'm tired.'

'Tired! What you doing last night, then?'

'Ah!' said the woman, wickedly. 'Give you three guesses.'

'One's enough,' said the man, and whispered something.

'Wrong!' cried the other, skittishly, jumping up. 'Shall us, then?'

'Yes! Let's!' And they departed into the dancing-room.

'I wish I could talk like that,' I said.

'I know exactly what she was doing last night,' said Phyllis, slowly. 'She was knitting socks in Eveleigh Gardens.'

'How do you know?'

'Because I was there. We dined with the Banburys.'

'Mary Banbury! Good heavens! So it was,' I cried. 'I knew I knew the voice. Good heavens!' I said again, shocked, I must confess.

'You were right,' said Phyllis. 'She's having an adventure.'

'Who with?'

'I couldn't see. He didn't *sound* much.'

'He sounded a little *too* much, I thought.'

'That's the worst of Mary. If she does do the right thing, she's bound to do it in the wrong way with the wrong people.'

'That's the worst of Puritans. When they

come off the pedestal they fall with such a bump. Let us go and inspect the adventurers.'

The lights had failed at one end of the dancing-room, which is long and narrow; and that end was in semi-darkness. As a result the usual dismal sobriety of the room was being relaxed, we found. For as we entered the Dark End I observed with astonishment that two, at least, of the couples passionately kissed each other. We danced on into the light, unscathed.

'It is odd, Phyllis,' I remarked, 'that in spite of my extreme regard for you, and in spite of the views which I expressed in a lift not long ago, I feel no temptation to salute you in that manner and in that place.'

'It *is* odd,' said Phyllis. 'You're a very inconsistent person, Mr Moon. There's Gordon!'

'And there's Mrs B! Just ahead.'

'Oh! Where?' cried Phyllis. 'Oh, yes! Isn't he *handsome?*' she breathed in my ear, very agreeably.

'Rather dashing,' I admitted.

'A nice moustache.'

'Too military.'

'Who *can* he be?' said Phyllis. 'They seem

to know each other very well.'

'They do,' I said, with my eye on the dancers. We passed on into the Dark End, just behind the adventurers.

'I wish you wouldn't push me backwards the whole time,' said Phyllis. 'I can't see.'

'It is odd,' I began, 'that you and I should be watching Mary B misbeha– Good heavens!'

'What's the matter?'

'I think,' I said, 'we had better go and sit out.'

We did.

'What was it?' said Phyllis again.

'Wild horses–' I began.

'It's all right,' she said, gravely. 'I'm afraid I've guessed. Oh, dear!'

Just then the music stopped and Mrs Banbury swam towards us, followed by the dashing stranger and, a little sulky, Mr Gordon Smith.

'Ah!' she cried, gay and unabashed, 'I was *wondering* if I should see you! You weren't here on Monday, were you?'

'I never dance on Monday,' I said, seriously. 'And if I did, I should keep it very dark. It is the beginning of the end.'

They sat down, and we were introduced. At least Mrs B mumbled at each of us, 'Do you know Mr–'; but it was clear enough that she did not know his name.

'Who is he?' I whispered presently, under cover of the young man's machine-gun conversation.

'Oh, I've met him here once or twice,' she said, vaguely, with a little toss of the head.

'Once or twice?' I echoed, raising my eyebrows.

Mrs B looked at me defiantly.

'Well, once,' she said. 'It was *your* fault.'

'I feel very guilty,' I said.

'So you ought,' said she, looking across at Phyllis.

'Not at all,' I said. 'I was thinking of you. Phyllis and I,' I added, 'are grown-ups.'

Mrs Banbury flushed, and looked away. Meanwhile the dashing stranger had produced what is known as a 'wad' of notes and was ordering costly refreshment, firing off a string of witticisms at the waiter as he did so.

It was now one o'clock. Two bottles of champagne and five plates of eggs and bacon were set before us. The young man paid for all.

Mr Smith became eloquent on the subject of police-raids.

'I hear a Scotland Yard man tried to get in

tonight,' he remarked, indignantly. 'Gave a member's name, they say, the tyke!'

'They saw his boots, I guess,' said the stranger, wittily, and Mrs Banbury laughed admiringly.

'It's a dirty trick,' said Mr Smith. 'Why can't they leave us alone?'

'Right, boy. One law for the rich and another for the poor – that's what it is. And after all, there's nothing wrong with this place, only that it breaks the law – eh?'

We all laughed heartily, and drank more champagne.

'Well, I hope they won't come tonight,' laughed Mrs Banbury.

'Don't you worry,' the stranger said. 'I know a bully little fire-escape if they do.'

'Phyllis,' I whispered, 'I have conceived a sudden distaste for this haunt of pleasure. Let us go.'

'Are you seeing yourself as others see you?' said Phyllis.

'No,' I said. 'I am seeing Mary as Mary sees us. Go and get your things, will you – and wait outside?'

'We're going, Mary,' I said, as Phyllis slipped away. 'Won't you come too?'

'Oh, not yet, Mr Moon!' Mrs Banbury protested.

'Sure? There might be a raid, you know.'

'Oh, nonsense! I'm just beginning to enjoy myself.'

'You can't go yet, you know,' said the stranger, with authority, looking at his watch. 'The night is young, my boy.'

'True,' I said. 'Very well, then. By the way, do you know Lady Burberry? I'd like to introduce you,' and seizing the young man by the elbow I led him across the room to a beautiful creature with the appearance of a mannequin, a complete stranger, I regret to say.

'Do you know Lord Ronald?' I said. 'Lord Ronald – Lady Burberry.' And I left them stammering at each other.

I stepped swiftly back and whispered three words in Mrs Banbury's ear.

'Rubbish!' she replied, but instantly took my arm and sailed with flying colour from the room.

Mrs Banbury, I think, has never spent so little time in a cloakroom.

'Damn it!' I said, halting halfway down the stairs, 'I've forgotten your partner.'

'That *brute!*' said Mrs Banbury. 'Don't speak of him!'

'Mr Smith,' I said.

'I forgot him too,' said she.

There was a great clamour above, and a door was slammed.

'Too late,' I said, and we passed on.

'Poor Mr Smith!' said Phyllis.

We all went the next day to see Mr Smith fined ten pounds as an 'illicit consumer.'

Mrs B's dashing friend gave his evidence with admirable clearness, and looked very well in his uniform.

'The beast!' muttered Mrs B, pallid under her veil. 'To pretend like that!'

'Be fair,' I said. 'I don't imagine it was all pretence – by any means. After all, the police are only human.'

Mrs Banbury blushed. I looked away. When I looked again she had raised her veil. Just the tiniest bit…

CHAPTER 7

The Compromise

It is not the part of a gentleman to gloat over the discomforts of a lady, however much she deserves it; and I am not the man to do it. I will say at once that I am very sorry about this affair.

Mary Banbury had behaved most strangely since the night at Boom's, when Phyllis and I found her losing her head with the dashing young detective who afterwards took part in the police-raid. Phyllis and I, on the other hand, have behaved most nobly. Never by a word or a look have we reminded Mary of the episode. Nor have we so much as hinted at it to others; we have even discouraged young Mr Smith from spreading about the tale.

And Mary, we supposed, was grateful. At any rate, she had shown a very new anxiety for our company, and treated us with a very new warmth. Phyllis and I were now one of her weekend party at 'Slings,' the Banburys' charming old house at Mortlake. It is a huge place on the south bank of the river, with a great walled garden full of magnificent trees behind it, a kind of country-house in town.

It was undeniably summer. A lazy breeze stirred in the tree-tops, but a haze of heat shimmered on the dry lawn. Phyllis and I sat in long chairs under the chestnut with long lemonades beside us, the water lily pond before us; and we watched Jack Banbury mowing the lawn beyond. And what is more pleasant than that? It is indeed a great delight to see the long smooth columns spread gradually across the grass; and as one smooth column succeeded another, one light, one dark, another light, another dark, we grew more and more pleased with ourselves. We even criticized when a column went a little wobbly.

Phyllis sighed suddenly.

'Another wobble!' she complained. 'Oh, dear! I feel as if in some way I was responsible for the lawn.'

'And *I* feel,' I said, 'as if I was doing the work myself. I get this feeling by lying back and watching Jack Banbury through half-closed eyes. Try it.'

'I will,' said Phyllis, sleepily. 'I can hardly keep my eyes open as it is'; and she tried it for some five minutes.

Phyllis looks very well with her eyes closed. One does not often see her so. And in a summer frock, with one hand behind her head and one soft arm in her lap, and her roguish lips demure and still for once, and a touch of the apple in her cheeks, and–

'I thought,' said Phyllis, suddenly opening her eyes, 'that you were going to try it too, Mr Moon.'

'I can hardly keep my eyes shut,' I said.

At this point Mary Banbury blew violently round the corner of the house, gave a flustered little cry, remarked 'I'm sorry,' and blew away again.

'Why are you sorry?' I called after her, but there was no answer.

'Have you noticed,' said Phyllis, reflectively, 'that Mary has become much more broad-minded recently – since Boom's?'

'I have observed with interest and gratitude that she positively flings us together, Miss Fair.'

'And *I* have observed that she deliberately arranges to leave us alone together – almost as if we were engaged, Mr Moon.'

'And then bursts in upon us – quite as if we were married.'

'You *are* married, Mr Moon.'

'She seems to have forgotten that. Do you know that during the past three days she has never once inquired when Angela and I are to be reunited?'

'It is extraordinary,' said Phyllis. 'And how sweet she is to us!'

'Extraordinarily sweet.'

'It may be,' Phyllis mused, looking at me very gravely, 'that her own indiscretion has made her more charitable to others. Not that we are indiscreet,' she added, looking at the pool.

'It *may* be so,' I said, looking at the sky.

'What else can it be?'

I made no reply.

'I hope you have no uncharitable thoughts, Mr Moon?'

I made no reply.

'You see,' continued Phyllis, 'she is just as sweet to everybody. Look how she flings Jean and Stephen together.'

'It's hardly the same thing,' I said. 'She wants Jean and Stephen to get engaged in her house. That's why she sent them off to the Dutch garden.'

'There she goes,' said Phyllis. And there was Mary's yellow sun-hat bobbing busily away under the limes.

'In the direction of the Dutch garden,' I

observed. 'It is Mary's fondest dream that before this weekend is over she will come round a corner and find Jean and Stephen in each other's arms. So, you see, Miss Fair,' I concluded, 'it's not at all the same thing.'

'I hope not, Mr Moon.'

Mrs Banbury, indeed, was making no secret of her matchmaking ambitions. Everyone had known for some time that Jean and Stephen were devoted to each other; but nothing, it seemed, would induce them to communicate the facts to each other – Stephen too frightened, and Jean too languorous to encourage him. They mooned about together, Stephen happily talking 'law-shop' and Jean happily dreaming about something else. They are an excellent match, for nobody without Jean's peculiar capacity for repose in all circumstances could possibly endure a life of Stephen's law-shop. But they would *not* advance. Their courting reminded me of the courting of newts, of which the female stands perfectly motionless, while the male poses in front of her, curiously contorting himself and lashing his tail, and generally suggesting immoderate affection, but never actually approaching her. To bring such a couple to 'the scratch' would indeed be a triumph for any hostess, and I well understood

Mrs Banbury's eagerness.

Jack Banbury came towards us, mopping his ruddy face. He is simple, hearty, and a stockbroker; the slave of his wife, and fond of practical jokes. He is entirely brainless; indeed, there is no harm in him of any kind, only that he has never grown up. Deplorably lacking in taste and delicacy of feeling, like his wife; but she ought to know better – Jack does not.

And, upon my word, when I contemplate the vulgarity and dullness of Jack I can almost forgive her for the excessive interest she shows in the affairs of other people.

'Well,' he said, breezily, lying flat on his broad back, 'and what's the betting now?'

'What's the event?' I inquired.

'The Marriage Stakes,' grinned our host. 'I've a level flyer with Fraser' (Fraser was another guest – an average-adjuster, and high in his profession) 'that Mary brings it off before tomorrow – and I wouldn't mind betting I lose my money,' he concluded, gloomily. 'Look at last night! What more could the man want? Dancing, a full moon, a hot night, cosy corners all over the garden, champagne, cress sandwiches, no dew on the lawn, and not another man so much as spoke to the girl. There they were, dancin', sittin' out, dancin', sittin' out, for four or five hours. And no further at the end of it than they were before!'

I glanced at Phyllis. Her eyes were closed. I half-closed mine. Jack's remarks are very often addressed to an audience of this kind.

'I tell you what,' he said, 'I've got an idea. For I'm damned if we don't fix things somehow tonight. Look here, my wife tells me the young man's full of old-fashioned Divorce Court notions, and, she says, if once he thought he'd compromised the girl he'd propose to her the next minute.'

'What do you mean by "compromise"?'

'Well, I mean, if he was found in her bedroom or something,' said Jack, crudely, 'like they are on the stage, you know!'

'Really, Jack,' I said, faintly, 'I must remind you that these two young lovers are your guests.'

'That would be compromising her,' he went on gaily, ignoring my remark, 'technically – though what harm he'd be likely to do when he hasn't even the courage to propose I don't quite know. The question is, *how* to get him into her bedroom?'

'Why not send him an invitation?' I asked, helpfully.

'Be serious, old man,' said my host. 'By the way, I suppose Miss Fair *is* asleep?' he added, anxiously.

'I certainly hope so,' I said, and we both examined Miss Fair. It seemed that she *was* asleep. 'But in case she's not, perhaps we'd better discuss some other aspect of the matter.'

Jack's only reply to this was to crawl across to me, and continue his remarks in a loud and penetrating whisper.

'Didn't you say you walked in your sleep sometimes?'

I nodded.

'Well, my idea is this, old man.' And thereupon he unfolded a crude and distasteful stratagem.

I was to pretend to walk in my sleep. Jack was to be aroused by my movements, and, frightened for my safety, summon Stephen Trout to assist him. Together they were to follow me, taking care, as tradition dictates, not to wake me. I was to lead them to Jean's room (to be fair to the man, the thing was to happen at an early hour, so that the girl would not be frightened), somnambulate into her room, followed by my protectors, and, passing out again, dreamily lock Stephen in (Jack undertook to see that the key was outside). Result, Jean and Stephen in compromising situation – door opened (by Jack) half an hour later and out steps Stephen dramatically, announcing engagement.

'You're no sport, Moon,' said my host, ruefully, when I had given my answer to this strange proposal.

Fortunately, just then, Phyllis woke up, and I gave no further thought to it. The evening passed quietly. Jean and Stephen walked up and down the lawn in the moonlight for some time, but when they came in it was evident that they were no more engaged than they were before. I reflected with satisfaction that Jack had lost his bet, and we all went to bed.

I had just turned my light out when there was a knock at the door, which was opened stealthily, and I heard in a whisper the words, 'Come on, Moon! Be a sport, old man!'

I opened my mouth to revile my host – and I thought better of it. I detest practical jokes, but I believe in an 'eye for an eye' in some things. I decided to be a sport.

I rose slowly out of my bed and stood at the side of it, muttering, while I slipped my feet into my bedroom slippers. Then, stretching out my arms in a groping manner, I stalked past Banbury into the dim corridor, and through my half-closed eyes I was glad to see that he had nothing on his feet.

'Capital, old man!' he chuckled. 'That's the stuff.'

'Shall I not throw it in the lake?' I replied, weirdly, and then, very rapidly, 'Where-is-my-hat-don't-send-me-away-Jane!'

I then turned to the left, and walked away with a brisk but, as I thought, an uncanny gait, Jack pattering behind. I went past Jean's room, past Phyllis' room, past the Banburys' room, past the bathroom, where I heard splashings, down the stairs and on to the front door, catching as I went a stealthy 'Wait a bit, old boy!'

As I was fumbling at the bolts Jack whispered, 'Steady on, old boy! This is no damn good! *Upstairs!*'

'The forest! The forest!' I answered bleakly. 'You shall not prevent me.'

So saying I stepped out and walked rapidly across the gravel-drive. A chilly night-breeze had come up with the tide, and the gravel, as I knew, is full of sharp flints, some of which I could feel even through my slippers. I was therefore glad to hear Jack running. He ran round in front and peered anxiously at me; I gazed at him with wide, unseeing eyes, not halting for an instant.

And I heard him mutter in a tone of awe to himself, 'Good God!'

He then fell in behind and followed me meekly back across the drive, uttering occasionally small sounds expressive of pain. At the front door I sheered off to the left again and recrossed the drive. Jack then, remembering apparently some casual scrap of information about sleep-walkers, assumed the voice of a Stronger Will, and, pointing to the house, said sternly, 'Go back, man! Go back to the house! Do you hear me?'

I paid no attention and passed on into the kitchen garden, where there is a bramble hedge, a very small path, and a great number of nettles. I walked round the kitchen garden four times, Jack groaning and cursing quietly behind, and occasionally turning on the Stronger Will.

Then, gathering speed, I rounded the house and made for the river; Jack gave a little yelp and began to run. Halfway to the river I began to feel chilly, so, turning sharply, I scurried back into the house and slipped for dear life up the back stairs, leaving Jack a long way behind.

Along the corridor I sleep-walked again, muttering a little, and for a very good reason. It seemed to me in the gloom that, as I approached, two of the doors were stealthily closed; it seemed to me also that I caught a glimpse of white and the suppressed chuckle of a lady.

So Mrs Banbury was in the Great Stratagem as well!

I became immediately the prey of one of those impish, hasty resolutions which afflict the best of us at times.

At the corner of the corridor I turned and waited. I saw Jack come up the stairs and disappear in the direction of Stephen's room, breathing heavily, no doubt to summon his aid in good earnest. This time the suspected door was quite certainly an inch or two ajar. I approached and firmly pushed it open. For I had decided that Mrs Banbury should play the part designed for Jean.

'For shame!' you remark. You are right.

The door resisted a moment only, and was softly closed behind me as I stalked across the moonlit room.

'Excuse-me-I-must-post-these-letters-I-must-post-them-soon,' I said rapidly, and turned.

The figure by the door made a faint giggling sound. I was surprised to see that she wore pyjamas – I had never thought of Mrs Banbury in pyjamas.

'You must be tired after all that walking, Mr Moon,' said Phyllis, softly.

'Good Lord!' I murmured. 'The wrong room! I'm awfully sorry, Phyllis.'

'I assume you are still asleep, Mr Moon?'

'Of course!'

'Then I have no complaint to make,' said Phyllis, calmly. 'Won't you sit down?'

'I'd better go–' and I moved towards the door.

'Too late,' she whispered. 'Sh!' There were voices outside – Jack's, 'He went along here,' and Stephen's, 'We mustn't wake him, whatever we do. There was a case once–,' and Mary's, just going on and on.

I sat down in the window, Phyllis on the bed. It would be indelicate to describe a lady in these circumstances, and I shall not do it. I will only say that her hair was down, and was much longer than I had imagined.

'I suppose you realize, Mr Moon,' said Phyllis, 'that you are "compromising" me?' And I'm afraid she giggled again.

'On the stage,' I replied, 'or in a court of law, this would certainly amount to a compromising situation. But then, of course, I am asleep.'

'Of course,' said Phyllis.

'And fortunately few of us conduct our-

118

selves as the law expects us to, even when awake.'

'Of course,' said Phyllis. 'At the same time, if Mary Banbury came in–'

'She would be delighted.'

'I'm afraid she would.'

There was a knock at the door.

'This,' I whispered, 'is becoming like a French farce.'

'There is one important difference, Mr Moon.'

'Yes?'

'The villain is asleep, Mr Moon. Stay quiet behind the curtain, Mr Moon.' And she opened the door.

Jean slipped in, with an armful of sponges, fresh, it seemed, from the bathroom. She embraced Phyllis, which is unusual, and informed her shyly, as a secret, that a marriage had been arranged between herself and Stephen Trout on the previous Friday evening.

The prescribed amount of kissing took place.

'But why a secret?' said Phyllis, at last.

'Well, we don't want Mary to be able to say she brought it off. Stephen says it would throw a shadow over the whole of our married life. We shall go to Scotland or somewhere and have a formal engagement there.'

'Poor Mary,' said Phyllis, chuckling. 'Well, I won't tell. And Mr Moon won't tell – because he's asleep.'

'Mr Moon?' said Jean, blankly. 'You may tell him if you like.' The dear creature!

Deeply moved, I left my curtain and, swaying towards the astonished girl, shook her warmly by the hand; and I said dreamily, 'Luck. Oh, luck! Poor Mary! Open the door, open the door, the forest.'

Jean opened the door, and stood behind it, in a frightened manner.

At that moment I heard the sound of the search party returning from the back stairs. Phyllis looked at me, and I looked at Phyllis with wide, unseeing eyes. Jean began hurriedly to close the door (Jean goes to too many French farces), but Phyllis stopped her.

'Stay there,' she whispered; then popped into the passage and cried mysteriously, 'Mary! Mary! Mr Banbury! Help!'

'Yes, dear,' piped Mrs Banbury, and the search party appeared in the doorway, carrying candles, and looking, I am bound to say, exceedingly ridiculous.

'It's Mr Moon,' whispered Phyllis. 'He's been standing there stock still for ten minutes, and I can't get him to move. I think he must be asleep.'

I stood stock still, with my chin tilted, faintly flapping my arms, and muttering. And through my wide, unseeing eyes I saw a look of unholy joy on Mrs Banbury's face.

'So *that's* where he went!' she said, advancing. 'How very curious! Poor child, you *must* have been frightened!'

'Oh, no!' said Phyllis. 'But I knew it was dangerous to wake him up. Don't talk too loud.'

'Leave him to me,' said Jack, and fixed his iron gaze upon me.

'Go-back-to-your-room,' he said invincibly. 'Go-back-to-your-room. Go-back–'

'The pig is black,' I murmured, 'the pig is black. But how much blacker is the sow, however,' I added, with a deep sigh.

Jack and Mary recoiled.

'Are you quite *sure* he's asleep?' said Mary, peering suspiciously and raising her voice, 'I don't believe he's asleep at all. Really, Mr Moon–'

'Sh!' said Phyllis.

'If you ask *me*, Phyllis,' said Mary, severely, still louder, 'this is all a piece of Mr Moon's– How long has he been here?'

'I'm quite *sure* he's asleep,' said a gentle

voice from behind the door. 'I've been watching him all the time.'

'*Jean!* You there too!'

They all turned; and through my wide, unseeing eyes I saw a look of great sadness on Mrs Banbury's face.

'Yes, wasn't it lucky, Mary?' said Phyllis in a kind of coo. 'I *might* have been frightened otherwise.'

'I remember,' began Stephen, 'there was a case once where a man committed a larceny in his sleep. It was held by the Divisional Court–'

'Look out!' said Phyllis. 'He's moving. Stephen's done it.'

Slowly, with dignity, groping before me, I passed out of the room, the party following me.

'Jean,' I muttered, halting at my door. 'Jean! Be careful. There is a plot. A plot. I cannot remember. Oh, dear!' And sighing heavily, I passed within.

'Well, if I were you, Phyllis,' I heard Mrs Banbury say, 'I should lock your door. You too, Jean.'

'I fancy Jean's is locked already,' said Phyllis sweetly. 'Isn't it, Mr Banbury?'

Mr Banbury made no reply.

'Poor Mary!' I said to myself.

CHAPTER 8

'Parallel Lines'

It was Friday, and a day big with destiny for many lives, as, indeed, all Fridays are. For we know that all Fridays are unlucky. Indeed, when I consider the number and variety of misfortunes recorded to have befallen my own friends on that ill-omened day I sometimes marvel that the human race as a whole should have so long survived a system which allows for a Friday every week. It is fortunate perhaps that we do not remember with the same fidelity of association those ills which fall on a Tuesday or a Wednesday; for otherwise the week would be scarcely supportable.

But there it is. We forget what happened on a Thursday, however unpleasant. But this was a Friday, and I shall never forget it. Perhaps in some unconscious struggle against the omens, I dined severely alone at the club; and when I saw young Mr Gordon Smith hovering towards me at the door I did not see him, but buried my face in the fourth page of an exceedingly modern novel, which I had read and re-read two or three times without blundering on the author's meaning.

After three weeks of bachelor independence the delight of reading at meals was as fresh as ever, and I read the page with satisfaction for the rest of dinner. At the desert, however, Mr Smith sidled up, and remarking, 'I say, do you mind if I–?' sat down. He was immaculate and handsome in white waistcoat and tails, and I do not think I looked better myself.

'Hullo!' I said, shutting my book with perfect breeding. 'Seen anything of Phyllis lately?'

The ancient Romans, we are taught, began a question with the word *Num* when they expected the answer 'No,' and with the word *Nonne* when they expected the answer 'Yes.' There is no record of what they said when they received the wrong answer.

'Yes,' said Mr Smith. 'I took her to Ascot yesterday.'

'Oh!' I said. My question had begun with *Num*.

'I've been thinking over your advice, Mr Moon,' he went on, stammering a little, 'some weeks ago. By Jove, it was at this very table, I believe!'

'Curious,' I murmured helpfully. I have seldom dined at any other table.

'You were right, of *course*,' he said.

'That's very gratifying. What was it I said?'

'*You* know – about Phyllis,' he said, earnestly. 'Not seeing so much of her these weeks, I've realized just what she is to me – just as you said.'

'And just what is she to you?'

'She's – she's' – the boy paused, fumbling for the exact, the poetical, the crumpling phrase – 'she's A1.'

'She is A1 to a good many people,' I said, wisely. 'I suppose Jean Renton's engagement made a good deal of difference? Have a glass of port.'

Mr Smith threw me a defensive look out of the corner of his eye, and gladly took refuge in the port.

'No,' he said. 'No, no. You were right about that too. I realized long ago that Jean wasn't quite– Of course, she's–' he continued lucidly. 'But she isn't really– If you understand me. I mean, I could never have felt for her– Not really, I mean– Not like Phyllis–'

'Well,' I said, 'I'm very glad.' And I believe I was. 'Are you dancing with her tonight?'

Again my question began with *Num*, but this time, I regret to say, it was betting on a certainty.

'No,' said Mr Smith. 'I tried to get her, but she's doing something else.'

'Is she?' I murmured, sympathetic.

'But I *am* dancing,' he continued, cheerfully, and then, with an anxious note, 'I say, you don't think it's rotten of me to go out with another woman, after – after what I've just said–'

'After your passionate avowal about Miss Fair? No, no, my boy. You're quite right to show your independence. Who is she?'

'She's a new friend,' he replied, with some satisfaction. 'Awfully fine woman. And the best dancer I know. Of course,' he added, 'she's much older than I am – at least, I should think so. It's not the same sort of thing, you know–'

'The same as what?'

'The same as, well – Phyllis.'

'Of course not.'

'But I like dancing, and she's such a good dancer – and–'

'And you like dancing with her?'

'That's it.'

'Of course,' I said, 'you're an expert. I'm not. But, if you are, I believe that the age and appearance of the partner is immaterial – it's the sheer artistic joy of doing the thing well. Youth and beauty don't count.'

'That's true,' said Mr Smith, with enthusiasm.

'Four feet that beat as one?'

'Yes,' he said, but with a dubious glance.

'Where are you going?' I asked, with a polite show of interest.

'I thought probably the "Thames".'

'Oh!' I said, with real interest. 'I shouldn't go there, would you? Not if you're going for the dancing. It's nice and quiet, of course, but the band's not good, is it?'

'Might be better, certainly.'

'Not a patch on the band at Boom's? Or "Spider's" either.'

'No.'

'And it's generally crowded – for dancing, I mean. Of course, if you just want to sit about and have a quiet supper–'

'Yes,' he said. 'Well, I'll see what she thinks. Goodbye, Mr Moon. Many thanks. See you again some time, I hope?'

'I hope so,' I said, but did not specify the time.

Halfway to the 'Thames' it became too clear that it was Friday.

'The taxi smells of petrol, Mr Moon,' said Phyllis, sniffing reproachfully.

'I am sorry, Miss Fair.'

'And is the driver extravagantly sober, Mr Moon?'

We reeled round an omnibus and chased an elderly gentleman on to the pavement.

'Not wildly, I think.'

Phyllis sighed.

'I wish you had a car, Mr Moon.'

'I hear you went to Ascot yesterday,' I remarked.

'Yes, Mr Moon. In a motor-car.'

'I seem to remember,' I said, mildly, 'inviting you to go somewhere yesterday – I rather forget where.'

'I think you intended travelling there by train, Mr Moon. I hate trains, Mr Moon. And taxis.'

'Tonight,' I said, 'you shall go home neither by train nor taxi, neither by tram nor omnibus nor car. I have a surprise for you.'

'I hate aeroplanes,' said Phyllis, yawning.

'I meant a boat.'

'A *boat*, Mr Moon?'

'A boat, Miss Fair.'

The 'Thames' is quite the most charming of the two or three clubs now dotted along the river of London, and I had formed a romantic and original plan. Both of us were again invited for the weekend to the Banburys' at Mortlake. The day before I had taken down my sailing dinghy, the *White Witch*, and moored her off the 'Thames'. There was a moon. It was fine. I proposed that after the dancing Phyllis and I should travel to Mortlake on the flood tide, a romantic sail (or possibly drift) in the moonlight.

I eloquently developed my ideas, and waited anxiously for the reply.

'I think I should want a chaperone for that,' said Phyllis.

To this astonishing remark I deemed it best to make no reply. After all, I am a married man.

We finished the journey in comparative silence, but for the yells of infuriated pedestrians which followed the taxi.

The 'Thames' is on the south bank, built in white stone, and from the river it looks like the villa of a Roman emperor, with a wide quadrangle which suggests a Roman bath. It is very quiet and sedate and clean. The band plays in a muffled, delicate fashion, soothing rather than exciting.

After two dances, performed by Phyllis with less than her usual gaiety, we went and sat in the court, the moon above us, the lights of London dancing across the river, the trams like lighted palaces swaying along the Embankment and swimming in the water. To our right the great dome of St Paul's hung in the sky, the ghost of a dome in the cloudy moonlight. It was very hot. The band played softly far away. I had no doubt that such an evening would drive away the black hags of Friday.

'I think I'm cross, Mr Moon,' said Phyllis, fanning herself.

'It would be a pity to be cross on a night like this.'

'If I'm not cross,' said she, 'I don't know what it is.'

'Perhaps it's Lo–' I began; and, just then, looking back through the windows at the dancers, I observed, with a satisfaction which I easily controlled, a familiar figure.

'There's Mr Smith,' I said.

'Oh, good!' said Phyllis, turning her head. 'I told him we were coming here.'

'Did you, indeed?' I answered, thoughtfully.

'Who's he with?'

'Someone we both know,' I answered, thoughtfully.

'I hope you're not jealous, Mr Moon. I hate jealousy.'

'Certainly not, Miss Fair. Why should I be?' There was no answer. 'Jealousy,' I went on, 'is quite alien from my character. I take the civilized view of these things.'

'What is that, Mr Moon?'

'Any common enthusiasm is known to be the surest ground for friendship. If Mr Smith and I were both devoted to Shakespeare this would help us to be firm friends. Logically there is no distinction between Shakespeare and a fascinating young woman. Logically, therefore, Mr Smith and I should be drawn together, as though by a common hobby–'

'A what, Mr Moon?'

'A common enthusiasm. And logically we should be able together to enjoy your society. Speaking for myself, I am perfectly ready to do so.'

'Are you, Mr Moon?'

'Euclid laid it down that things which are equal to the same thing are equal to one another. *He* knew.'

'Didn't he also say,' said Phyllis, quietly, 'that two parallel lines should never meet?'

'True,' I said. 'But it was you who told Mr Smith that we were coming here. Hullo!'

Mr Smith stood beside us with a lady. I shook hands warmly.

'Hullo!' he said. 'Do you know Miss Isabel

Gay?' And he presented me to my dear wife Angela.

This has happened once or twice before in the course of a Bachelor Moon, though the circumstances of the present introduction were perhaps peculiarly unfortunate – unfortunate, I mean, for Mr Smith. Isabel Gay is my wife's old stage-name, and when she is Isabel she wears a golden wig (with fringe) and the wonderful blue dress in which she made her hit as Dolly Traddles in *The Purple Patch*. She looks dazzling.

The rule is strict on these occasions that her incognito must be preserved, so far as possible. Phyllis knows the rules, and gave her an affable smile, which Angela did not seem to see. To Mr Smith Phyllis gave the hundredth part of a curt nod.

'How d'you do?' said Angela sweetly. 'I think we've met before, Mr Moon.'

'I believe we have,' I answered, gravely. 'May I have a dance, Miss Gay? I dare say Mr Smith and Phyllis would like to have a talk.'

For reasons of my own I believe the talk, *as a talk* was a failure, though all that I caught as we went inside was the one word 'Well–' uttered in a tone, of challenge, not to say reproach. The word was uttered by Phyllis.

I much enjoyed my dance with my wife, and I remember that I clapped for an encore at the close of each instalment.

'How is Mrs Moon?' said my partner, after a while. 'I've heard so much about her.'

'She is *looking* extremely well,' I said.

'I expect you'll be glad to see her again,' said Angela, smiling.

'I shall,' I said. 'In ten days now.'

'Not earlier?'

'It rests with her.'

Angela smiled again.

'I dare say she's enjoying herself.'

'It's conceivable,' I said, as the dance ended. 'By the way, if you *should* happen to see her—'

'Yes?'

'You might assure her that I'm behaving splendidly.'

'I'm sure you are, Mr Moon.'

We joined the others.

Phyllis, I observed, sat in much the same pose of remote and subtle discontent as she had had before the arrival of Mr Smith; as for Mr Smith, he looked crumpled. I was quite sorry for Mr Smith.

Mr Smith took me aside and stammered at me in a corner. Mr Smith reads too many novels.

'I'm awfully sorry, Mr Moon,' he began. 'Really I am – I'd no idea–'

'What about?' I asked, in a fog.

'About your wife. I'd no idea. Really, I–'

'That's all right, my boy,' I said, magnanimously.

'I thought she was a widow – really, I did–'

'Of course,' I said. 'Anyone would. Whatever's the matter?'

'You're sure you're not annoyed?' he said, relieved. 'Phyllis seemed to think– I don't quite understand why–'

'Ah!' I shook my head. 'I shouldn't try, my boy. These women! She *does* dance beautifully, doesn't she?'

Mr Smith grinned, and we shook hands – the Lord knows why.

We joined the others and sat in silence for some time.

'It's a glorious band,' said Phyllis, primly, at last, as the music began again.

'I think it's *too* awful,' said Angela.

After another silence Angela shivered a little, and Phyllis said solicitously. 'Wouldn't you like a wrap, Miss Gay? You look cold.'

This, it seemed, was an offensive observation; for Angela said, shortly but sweetly, 'I'm warm as a toast, thank you,' and looked colder than ever. She also added, 'You're looking tired, my dear.'

Not liking the tone of this conversation I said breezily, 'Well, my lad, we mustn't waste our time, must we?' and shuffled my feet as if about to rise.

'Shall we dance, Gordon?' said Angela, brightly.

Mr Smith looked timidly at Phyllis, and sheepishly at me. He then led Angela sheepishly away. Poor Mr Smith!

The tide was making up. A tug swished lazily past, winking one red eye at us.

'Still cross?' I murmured at last.

'Not with you,' said Phyllis, surprisingly, and turned upon me a sweet and melting smile; and if you understand this change of air you know more about the creatures than I do.

'Poor Mr Smith,' I said, gently. 'He only wanted a dance.'

'If you think I'm jealous–'

'Certainly not. You thought better of him – that's all.'

Phyllis smiled, but said nothing.

'It's just as well,' I said, 'you don't think better of me. Shall we dance?'

'Or shall we go?' said Phyllis. 'Do you know, John, I rather like the idea of your "surprise". How lovely it looks on the water!'

'A little awkward – now – isn't it?' I ventured, cautiously.

'Awkward, Mr Moon?'

'We may be seen, you know.'

'I should rather like young Gordon to see us,' said Phyllis, with strange intensity. 'As for you, Mr Moon, I thought you didn't mind what anyone said about you–'

'I wasn't thinking of "anyone",' I replied.

'Of course if you're *afraid*, Mr Moon–'

'What about your chaperone, Miss Fair?'

'Damn the chaperone,' said Phyllis, surprisingly, and then with great energy, 'Think what fun we'd have escaping, John – all stealthily – showing no lights! Oh, do let's!' And she laid an appealing, friendly, impulsive little hand on my arm.

And then, even as madness must have possessed Mr Smith that Friday, a madness came upon me.

'I wish,' I said, 'that you and Angela could be friends.'

'But, of *course*,' said Phyllis, 'I think she's wonderful. I adore her,' she added.

'Real friends,' I persisted (I have heard Phyllis adore soda-water). 'It's the same story – things which are equal to the same thing, you know–'

'Parallel lines,' murmured Phyllis.

'Here you are,' I continued, warming to my theme, 'two first-class creatures – in very different ways, of course – and, to use your own expression, I adore the two of you–'

'In very different ways, of course,' said Phyllis.

'Exactly. And what distresses me is that you *don't* adore each other. Look how Smith and I get on together. But you women–'

'But we *do*, John,' said Phyllis, gazing over the water. 'Anyhow, *I* do. There's another tug. Oh, do let's go!'

I nerved myself, and said insanely: 'Well, shall we ask Angela to come?'

There was a dreadful little pause.

'Very well, John,' said Phyllis; then, very quietly, 'Let's.'

'No,' I said, emphatically, the madness lulled in me by that quiet, obedient voice. 'You're perfectly right. We won't.' I looked at my watch. 'Twelve o'clock! Thank heaven, Friday's over! Come along!'

'What fun!' said Phyllis, and we stole away.

We stole away from the haunts of revelry, got our 'things,' crept through the secretary's office to the steps, where the *White Witch* lay in the shadow, and hoisted sail, 'All stealthily,' and trying not to laugh.

There was a light breeze from the southwest, and we pushed off gaily to the sound of a waltz, for we had to pass the dancing room and the quadrangle, and I steered straight out into the river, but the breeze was off-shore and we drifted past very close, on the tide.

'I think,' whispered Phyllis, 'that's Gordon on the wall. And there's someone on the steps.'

'Poor Mr Smith!' I whispered.

'Is that you, Robin?' came a clear, sweet voice over the water. 'May I come too?'

A strange remark escaped my companion.

'Of course, my dear,' I answered, and putting the tiller over I made for the steps.

'I'm all ready,' said Angela, stepping in. 'I noticed the boat as soon as I got here. Goodbye, Gordon – you'll meet me at the Bridge?'

Mr Smith, dimly discernible, said nothing. I pushed the boat off again.

'*Isn't* this fun, Phyllis?' said Angela.

'Isn't it?' said Phyllis.

And what happened after that, as the Colonel of Marines remarked, is another story.

Oh, Lord!

CHAPTER 9

A Mysterious Affair At 'Slings'

'Damn!' I said, and sneezed thirteen times.

At the seventh sneeze the brown squirrel dropped his nut, flashed along a bough, leapt into another tree, and disappeared.

High up in the great oak tree at the bottom of the Banbury's lawn there hangs a red silken hammock, some twenty feet from the ground. Below the tree is a kind of arbour, bounded on three sides by a high box-hedge, which hides it from the house, and on the fourth by the water-lily pond, where goldfish of a singular obesity and redness float languidly among the water-lilies, like aldermen in Paradise.

From the hammock (which I believe to be unsafe, as it is certainly the worst possible place for hay-fever, because of the acacia tree across the arbour) one can see above the hedge the old house and the rich green lawn, and, beyond, that leafy reach of the river which winds up towards Strand-on-the-Green. And here it is my delight to lie upon a hot Sunday afternoon (hay fever or no), to feed the squirrels with nuts, to gaze through the leaves at tiny corners of blue sky, to compose the plots of many novels, to reject them all as hardly worth the labour of writing, to think great thoughts, and reflect upon the past.

At the moment, through the leaves, I could see (but unseen) Mr Gordon Smith with Phyllis strolling on the lawn. I could also see from time to time Mrs Banbury's face at an upper window, where she would glance at the two strollers, hover for a moment, and withdraw. I had no doubt that Mary Banbury was matchmaking again.

These things caused me to reflect upon the past. I reflected on the strange circumstances in which Phyllis and I had arrived at that house on Friday night (or rather Saturday morning). It will be remembered, or if it is not, I now inform you, that we left the Thames Dancing Club by boat at about one o'clock, my dear wife Angela, Phyllis, and myself. The night was fine, the moon shone, with a light but rising breeze from the southwest. We slipped away merrily towards Westminster, rippling through the smooth, dark water, remote and lonely in the shiny twilight of midstream; the water might have been the water of an Italian lake, the lighted city on our right some ancient capital of the Indies. Westminster Bridge rose up before us, thrilling and tremendous, and the great tide swept us through, swishing awfully about the piers. The long black reaches of Lambeth and Vauxhall lay before us, inhospitable, lightless, but indubitably thrilling. And in my foolish mind I thought again, 'Surely, surely, in such a scene these two dear excellent creatures may be *drawn* together and become dear one to another, as they are to me!'

I will not at length describe that voyage. I will not apportion blame, I will only confess again that I was foolish, and pass on as quickly as may be.

We did not speak often. Angela expressed the opinion that I should strike the central pier of Westminster Bridge if I did not alter course. Phyllis thought I had plenty of room to spare. She was right. Phyllis, a little later, admired the appearance of the Houses of Parliament. Angela thought they looked better by day. Angela at Lambeth remarked that it was growing chilly. Phyllis, on the other hand, was as warm as a toast.

Sometimes I ventured to draw attention to

a star, a shadow on the water, a factory against the sky; when both my companions eagerly assented that it was beautiful. Above me in the heavens I saw the twin stars of Castor and Pollux, the friends of the mariner, but as we passed into the Vauxhall Reach I felt that tonight they watched my bark with no protecting eyes – nay, nor Venus neither.

Angela was right about the cold. A black, fat cloud had covered the moon; the breeze had risen suddenly to a wind, as it does in these waters, and in Vauxhall Reach we found ourselves in a rough sea.

The *White Witch* sped on gallantly into the night. She is a 'wet' boat, though noble, and off the Biscuit Works she plunged her nose into a great wave and flung a quantity of spray over my guests. And for all my care she did this again and again at varying intervals from Vauxhall Reach to Chelsea Bridge.

Let us haste. During this half-hour we spoke but seldom, and the conversation followed the general lines already indicated. It was Angela, I think, who first expressed the view that the whole expedition was ill-judged and rash; Phyllis, I fancy, who said that for such an adventure it was a small thing to become soaked to the skin in evening dress and a thin wrap. Up the long Chelsea Reach, however, both wind and wave increased, and at the Bridge, where Mr Smith was waiting in the car for Angela, I fancied that there was no longer any difference of opinion between them. And I expected them both to join Mr Smith with alacrity. Angela indeed implored Phyllis to go with her, and they kissed each other several times, as those who understand each other. My object was gained, I felt; I had drawn them together.

But Phyllis, to the general astonishment and concern, obstinately refused to leave the boat. She would not be beaten, she said. She had put her hand to the plough. She would finish the journey. And it was so. So Mr Smith and Angela drove away, not saying much.

The wind, as it happened, abated very soon; and we sailed without incident as far as Putney, where the wind fell, and a thin drizzle of rain; and from there we took a tow from a friendly tug.

There was no more moon, nor any shadow or romance or sentiment. Phyllis spoke seldom, though then without reproach or hint of displeasure. But there was wrapped about her and about the boat a forgiving sweetness, a settled melancholy that was not wholly satisfactory. But she neither shivered nor so much as admitted she was wet.

So we came, at about 3 a.m., to the shores of 'Slings' at Mortlake.

And there in the summer-house sat Mr Smith and Mrs Banbury, waiting for us, and Mrs Banbury with the well-known martyr's look of those who sit up through the night, waiting for others.

'Thank God!' she murmured, kissing Phyllis. 'I didn't know *what* to think.'

'But why *ever* did you wait up?' said Phyllis, amazed. 'You never have before.'

'You never came home in a *boat* before,' said Mary (as one might say, 'You never came home in a bed before'). 'My poor dear! Why *didn't* you let Gordon drive you back?'

'We didn't know he was coming here,' said Phyllis, truthfully.

'Of course you didn't,' said Mary, archly. 'I remember now. It was to be a "surprise".'

'A surprise for whom?' I murmured.

'The less *you* say, Mr Moon, the better,' said Mrs Banbury.

Yes, there was little doubt that Mary had a new stratagem afoot.

And now, tired of sneezing, I closed my eyes and composed myself for sleep; for a man can do many things in his sleep, but it will be generally conceded that sneezing is not one of them.

I dreamed of I know not what, and I would not be so inconsiderate as to tell you, if I knew. I woke to the sound of a voice I knew – a man's voice, earnest, eloquent, emotional.

'I have loved you from the very first moment I saw you,' said the man. 'That day at Haverstock – do you remember?'

Mr Smith's voice.

'I remember,' said a girl's voice, softly.

The voice of Phyllis.

When a gentleman through no fault of his own finds himself a witness at another man's proposal of marriage there is only one thing a gentleman can do – sit still and pretend he is not there. Had it been the secret converse of two financiers I should have warned them of my presence; but I could hardly lean out of the hammock and cry, 'Hi! Stop proposing! I'm listening!' On the other hand, determined though I was to treat whatever I heard as confidential, I did not see why I should deny myself the entertainment of hearing more. I wriggled cautiously on to my stomach and peered down through the network at the head of the hammock.

Mr Smith was sitting on the garden-seat, immediately below me, very close to Phyllis, who sat in a most uncharacteristic pose, with her chin on her breast. Mr Smith held one of her hands in his, and I judged from his attitude that he did not know what to do with it.

'You wore that blue hat, I remember,' he continued, passionately. 'We walked through the woods to Bellinger; and I thought then, as I have thought ever since, "If there is one woman on God's earth to whom I was meant to join my life, that woman walks beside me".'

Strange how the passion of love can inflame the dullest of us beyond our natural powers. I had no idea that young Mr Smith could so select or deliver his words.

Phyllis raised her lovely head, and looked at him in the eyes. I know that look.

'Do you ask me to believe that?' she said gravely.

'There has never been anyone else,' he answered, fearlessly meeting her gaze.

The dog! I thought. What about Jean Renton? What about Marigold? And what, ah! what about that red-haired minx I've heard about?

I had a monkey-nut in one hand; for two

pins I would have dropped it on the lad.

For Phyllis, it seemed, knew naught of these things.

'You make me very proud,' she said gently. 'But–'

I sighed. I had never before seen Phyllis quite so solemn. I had said so many beautiful things to her; and none of them, that I could remember, had made her very proud. No, I was not jealous. I simply sighed.

'Let there be no "but's",' cried the boy; and now he seized both her hands and worked them up and down, as you may see men work the beer-handles in our houses of refreshment. 'Oh, my dear, won't you put me out of my suspense? You are my hope, my dream, life has no other meaning for me but you. You are my first thought when I wake, my last before I sleep. I cannot face the years without you – tell me, tell me if there is any hope–'

I rubbed my eyes, scarce recognizing this burning suitor.

Phyllis shook her head with an air of tragical doubt.

'Tell me, at least, if there is anyone else–' said the youth.

'There is no one else,' she said, decidedly, and I felt that she was won at last.

Then she said casually, 'I think you'd better kiss my hand now.'

I rubbed my eyes again; this was a most extraordinary Phyllis.

'Right-o,' said her lover, surprisingly. 'Where shall I begin?'

'You make me very proud,' she said softly. 'But–'

'Let there be no "but's"!' said Mr Smith, and then at last the light broke on my bewildered and no doubt obtuse intelligence. The young things were acting. This was a rehearsal of Mrs Banbury's mysterious 'entertainment' for Sunday evening – or part of it. Also, no doubt, it was an ingenious part of Mrs Banbury's matchmaking campaign. And I was not spying on an emotional scene at all.

You *may* think that I was disappointed by a *bathos* so profound. You wrong me. I was glad – glad, of course, that my eavesdropping mattered so little. I mean no more.

And glad, I reflected, that Mrs Banbury's little entertainment would not be a surprise for me, after all. I had a suspicion that it had been intended as a very particular surprise for me.

I felt the more sure of this as I watched the progress of the little play below me, which was now approaching its climax. The exact point of the drama I forget, if indeed I ever discovered it; but at a certain point it became necessary for Mr Smith to put his arm round Phyllis and salute her with a stage kiss on the lips. The young man placed his face about nine inches from hers, and shyly laid a hand on her shoulder. I even saw his lips move; and if you have ever seen a stage kiss from immediately above, you may understand just how ridiculous they looked.

But even then, and how much more that evening, when I sat with Mrs Banbury in the stalls, I seemed to penetrate that busy mind; and I understood that that same genius which had selected that particular drama (by the dramatist James Overton) and those two particular actors, would exhibit a subtle pleasure from my presence in the audience during that particular scene.

In point of fact it left me cold.

The actors, I observed, both blushed a little.

The rehearsal was over at last. Mr Smith remarked, 'Well, that ought to be all right,' and Phyllis said, 'Yes, Gordon, you're splendid,' and withdrew a little along the bench.

I was just about to clap my hands or in

some way advertise my presence, when my attention was drawn to the strange conduct of Mr Smith. He sat bolt upright, very carefully pulled taut his old Etonian tie, glanced nervously to every corner of the arbour and even behind him at the impenetrable hedge, placed his finger inside his collar and pulled as if it were choking him, again tightened his tie, glanced nervously at Phyllis, and away again, kicked a stone, cleared his throat and remarked:

'I say, Phyllis?'

'Yes, Gordon?'

'I've got something to say to you.'

'Yes, Gordon?'

This time I was more intelligent, and I knew exactly what Mr Smith had to say. But, shameless yet, I did not shut my eyes, I did not stop up my ears. For I was consumed with curiosity to know how he would say it. Would he borrow from the dramatist James Overton? Would he use him as a stalking-horse, with a sly quotation here, a subtle allusion there? Would he go one better?

Or what?

Mr Smith adjusted his tie and edged with an air of infinite boldness an inch nearer to Phyllis. Her hands lay inviting in her lap. He did not take them. He did not take one of them.

He said, 'I say, Phyllis–'

'Yes, Gordon?'

'I wonder if – I mean, do you think you could ever–'

Alas! Where now was that rolling eloquence, that easy choice of words? Poor fool, I thought, give her a slice of the excellent Overton!

Phyllis, tired of saying, 'Yes, Gordon?' said nothing.

'The fact is, Phyllis,' said the unhappy youth, kicking the ground. 'I mean – Oh, damn it! I don't know how to say it–'

Poor Mr Smith. And he *did* look so handsome.

'It's awful cheek, I'm afraid,' he continued. 'But could you ever – well, *you* know what I mean–'

Phyllis received this somewhat contestable assertion in a thoroughly merciful and sensible manner.

'I suppose I do, really, Gordon,' she said, with a very sweet smile. I could not see it, but I know it was sweet.

Mr Smith eagerly thrust one very brown hand towards her, and laid it on the seat.

'How topping of you!' he said. 'You *are* a

brick. And you don't mind?'

'I don't *mind*,' said Phyllis, 'but–'

And now surely was the suitor's chance. 'Let there be no "but's"! I cannot face the years…' and so forth. Confound it, he had the whole thing in his head!

What Mr Smith said, ruefully, was: 'But there's someone else, I suppose?'

'No – no – but– Well, I can't tell you now, Gordon, not today. I'd like to think about it.' She rose. 'But will you promise to ask me again, Gordon? And, Gordon,' she finished, mischievously, 'will you ask me better next time?'

'You darling!' said Mr Smith, suddenly inspired. 'I'm a fool, I know,' and falling on his knees upon the gravel path he reverently kissed her hand.

At that moment, I am sorry to say, by the purest accident, the monkey-nut slipped from my excited fingers and fell upon the back of his neck. Phyllis glanced aloft, but said nothing. Mr Smith was too much moved to notice.

Mr Smith rose, with two damp patches on his spotless flannels, turned on his heel, and left the arbour.

Phyllis stood in thought for half a minute, then, turning her face up, a face all twinkles in the shadow, she whispered: 'You can come down now, Mr Moon.'

I climbed down silently, and took Mr Smith's corner of the seat.

'It only shows,' I said, 'the superiority of Art to Nature.'

'What does, Mr Moon?'

'Poor Mr Smith!' I said. 'Why didn't you have him? No man can be intelligent when he is proposing marriage.'

'Why not, Mr Moon?'

'It is not an intelligent action,' I replied. 'All the same I am glad you insist on style in your love-making.'

'Naturally,' said Phyllis. 'After all your – your conversation, Mr Moon, naturally I do.'

'How naughty you are today, Miss Fair!'

Phyllis handed me a monkey-nut.

'*That* was very naughty of *you*, Mr Moon.'

'*That* was a squirrel,' I said. 'Poor Mr Smith! I was quite disappointed.'

'I will not be engaged on Mary's premises,' said Phyllis very firmly, pursing her lips.

'How very rude,' I said, with great delight.

At this moment there was a step on the path, and Mary Banbury put her head round the corner.

'Hullo!' she said, with ill-concealed surprise. 'I thought Gordon was here.'

'He was,' said Phyllis, looking at the ground, in a tone most lugubrious, as one who has been through a sad and shattering scene.

Mrs Banbury gave me a long look. Such a look! Then she departed without another word.

'Was that quite nice?' I asked, after a short time.

'One up,' said Phyllis, twinkling. 'All the same, Mr Moon, I believe I should have had him; only–'

'Only what, Miss Fair?'

'Only I knew you were there, Mr Moon,' said Phyllis. 'So did Gordon,' she added.

'*What?*' I cried. 'Then the proposal was a fake?'

'Perhaps, Mr Moon.'

'I don't believe you, Phyllis.'

'You're very rude, Mr Moon.'

And to this day I do not know the truth of it.

CHAPTER 10

Virtue Rewarded

I woke with that sensation of well-being and contentment which is only enjoyed by a poor man waking in the houses of the rich. My clothes neatly folded on a chair, the shining can of hot water, the chaste clean towel which draped it, the obvious 'guest-liness' of the room (the wisteria-pattern on the walls and the little shelf of holy books) – these things renewed in me the sense that I was a person of importance, and in the hands of friends who valued me at my worth. Outside I could see trees, and on them the sunlight; a few birds sang un-obtrusively, not with that full-throated, rich, and senseless clamour which hails the dawn. It was long past the dawn. At home my clothes would have been on the floor in a heap; at the club there would have been no trees; here there was everything. And this was right and just; for I am a man who *ought* to have everything.

I savoured these sensations luxuriously, as men do at the end of a holiday. And indeed the Bachelor Moon was over. Tomorrow I was to return to my home and my dear wife Angela. And I was glad. The club had long since been hateful to me (but for the week-end hospitality of the Banburys I should have felt like taking rooms); I seemed to have done extremely little work (the writing of brilliant irresponsible masterpieces – which is my profession – requires above all a settled humdrum routine of life); my wardrobe was in a sad state of incompleteness; I had lost my nail-scissors; on such nights as I had no engagements I had been for two weeks a prey to loneliness; it would be pleasant to be settled at home with my wife Angela again, to sit together in the evenings and argue happily about every-thing; to taste afresh the various joys of marriage, all old squabbles forgotten and a brand-new life ahead of us. In a word, so far as I was concerned, the Bachelor Moon had justified itself again. We always say that after every Bachelor Moon we have a honey-moon. Absurd creatures...

Nonetheless, when I thought of Phyllis–

Nonetheless, I was going to say, I determined that this day should be a very good day. I stepped carefully out on the right side of the bed.

I enjoyed my bath, and in my mind entirely reorganized Jack Banbury's bathroom; and in the bath I sang, loudly and with emotion, as a man having a good conscience and glad to be alive. I shaved with less than the usual reluctance, but, shaving, reflected that after tomorrow, though I might not see Phyllis so frequently, I should shave after breakfast, and not before. Sometimes after lunch. I dressed – but I will not pretend that I remember what I wore. I dressed, I know.

Breakfast was a happy little affair. Is there another thing that so sets off the lives of the rich as breakfast? Is there another thing that so justifies the existence of a rich and leisured class as the pleasure of a poor man in breakfasting once or twice after their daily custom? Not to be confronted with a single egg supported by a single rasher, predestined, unavoidable; but to see upon an ancient dresser a choice, a *row*, of many mysteries, all familiar but all fresh and strange, to raise in turn each thrilling cover and not to decide on anything till the whole have been considered, to mix fish with bacon, and sausages with egg, the bacon marvellously crisp, the fish-cakes miraculously savoury and warm – but there–

There was no one in the dining-room. But Phyllis came in like the early morning through the window and poured out my tea.

'Everybody gone?' I asked; for it was Monday, and the end of the party.

'Yes,' said Phyllis. 'But Mary hopes we'll stay on till tea-time, anyhow. But we shall have to amuse ourselves, she says.'

'Curious,' I said, munching, 'I wonder why Mary keeps on inviting me here, when she hardly ever sees me, Miss Fair.'

'Why do you keep on accepting, Mr Moon?'

I waved my hand at the sideboard. 'Besides,' I said, 'it amuses me to feel that I'm in constant danger.'

'What is the danger, Mr Moon?'

'I don't quite know, Miss Fair. Why wasn't Mr Smith invited this time?'

'I think she's abandoned that idea,' said Phyllis, coyly.

'Curious,' I said, as I approached the dresser for the third time, not because I wanted more food but purely to enjoy the sensations of opulence. 'However, away with such thoughts! This is our last day.'

'You mean – *your* last day, Mr Moon,' said Phyllis, with an air of unconcern. '*I* didn't have kidney and kedgeree together, Mr Moon. Nor scrambled eggs and cold pheasant, Mr Moon.'

'*Our* last day,' I repeated. 'And must be celebrated specially, like all the great religious festivals, by eating a great deal of unusual food. But apart from that, Phyllis, what are your views about the spending of a perfect day?'

'To begin with, I should be very careful about my company,' said Phyllis, taking a large pear. 'I thought of ringing up Gor–' but the rest of Mr Smith she buried in the pear.

'Mr Smith,' I replied, 'to give him the name which Providence in its wisdom designed for him – Mr Smith has a whole life of you before him, that is, if you insist on becoming Mrs Smith – Mrs Smith,' I repeated dreamily, savouring the sound of it. 'Mrs Smith–'

'Go on, Mr Moon,' said Phyllis, with the faintest hint of impatience.

'But I have only this one day. It is therefore my right to choose the company. I choose you. You, if you like, may choose weapons and place. No seconds, of course.'

'I choose the lawn,' said Phyllis, 'if you've quite finished eating. There is still a little marmalade and kidney left, Mr Moon.'

'Your choice of weapon is ignoble, Miss Fair,' I said, rising with dignity. 'The place is better.'

Under the extreme skirts of the great chestnut, pleasantly half in the shade and half in the sun, which is the secret of life, I luxuriously filled my pipe. Phyllis watched me curiously.

'You talk very prettily,' she said at last. 'But you know that's all you care about really.'

'Talk, Miss Fair?'

'Smoke, Mr Moon.'

'It's much the same thing.'

'Then could you give up an hour's smoke for an hour's talk with – with, shall we say, Miss Fair?'

'There is no talk without a flame,' I murmured, vaguely.

'Gordon never smokes when he is talking to me,' said Phyllis, after a short silence.

'At his age,' I said, 'boys often find it difficult to do both at the same time.'

'You are evasive, Mr Moon. Let me put it this way. If you had the choice between never smoking again, and never seeing, shall we say, Miss Fair again – which would you choose?'

160

'The question is misconceived,' I answered, puffing happily. 'I shall always enjoy my pipe. I shall never enjoy Miss Fair.'

'I beg your pardon?'

'It is granted. You are right to this extent, however. There is one thing only that can stop a healthy man from smoking–'

'And that is?'

'That is love, Miss Fair.'

'But not after breakfast, I suppose?'

'Not too soon after breakfast,' I corrected.

'Gordon,' began Phyllis, 'never smokes till after lunch–'

'Gordon ought not to smoke at all,' I said. 'But shall we talk less about Gordon? You may remember it is my last day.'

'You said I might choose the weapons.'

'Mr Smith is not a civilized weapon,' I said. 'However, let us talk about him if you wish. Him and Mrs Smith. Mr and Mrs Smith. "Among those present were Mr and Mrs Smith"... "The guests included Mr and Mrs–"'

'Gordon Smith.'

'Not to be confused with Mr and Mrs Lennox Smith. Or Mrs Trevor Smith. How strange and thrilling it will be to receive the first letter from "Phyllis Smith." Or "Phyllis Gordon Smith." And for you, how sweet to

161

give up the name of Phyllis Fair. All for love. *What* a–'

'*Pax!*' said Phyllis, blushing a little. 'I won't mention him again. But you are a brute, Mr Moon.'

'I am,' I admitted. 'But then,' I sighed, 'it is my last day.'

'Well,' said Phyllis, 'and what would you like to do? I am at your service – for one day.'

'Let us lie on the lawn, to begin with. This seat is hard. It is a theory of mine,' I continued, 'that every man, whatever his occupation, should from time to time do one or two of those simple elemental things which belong to all the ages and all the races of man. Such as singing, and dancing, and drinking wine; and he should follow one of the ancient enduring sports, such sports as have a spice of danger about them, such as hunting, sailing, or riding a horse. And, of course, Love,' I added, casually. 'For these things remind him that after all he is only a man and vulnerable. They keep him humble, and at the same time healthy.'

'You have forgotten eating,' said Phyllis.

'And, of course, eating. And it follows that, as a man's life, so should a man's last day include some of these pleasures. Now where shall we begin?'

'You've begun already,' said Phyllis. 'You sang in your bath.'

'Byron. Converted by the genius of a female composer into an incredibly sentimental song. I like it. Listen.' And I sang:

So we'll go no more a-roving
So late into the night,
Though the heart be ne'er as loving
And the moon be ne'er as bright.

'"So we'll go no more a-roving",' I repeated. 'Extraordinarily sad and fitting. Well, what is to follow?'

'I don't mind watching you eat again,' said Phyllis.

'Then there is Love, of course,' I said, casually.

'You've chosen to smoke instead, Mr Moon.'

I knocked out my pipe.

'But I didn't mean–' said Phyllis hastily. 'Please have another, Mr Moon.'

'I often sit and think,' I said, putting my pipe away, 'with ill-concealed surprise, how virtuous I am and how little I get for it.'

'Virtue is its own reward, Mr Moon.'

'And is it worth it at the price?' I mused.

'Tomorrow, for example, I return to my wife, after a month of virtue, principally spent with you. And what is my reward?'

'If you think it virtuous, Mr Moon,' said Phyllis, with some spirit, 'to monopolize me for a month and then go back to your wife – I may observe,' she added, 'that I have no wife.'

'But you have your virtue, Miss Fair, which, as you say, is its own reward.'

Phyllis screwed up her nose in an odd way.

'Yes,' I mused, regarding her curiously. 'We men are the slaves of convention. You, I suppose, Miss Fair, in a suitable case, would give up everything for love?'

'Naturally, Mr Moon. Any woman would. Not too soon after breakfast,' she added hastily.

'You believe, I dare say, that one should snatch at life with both hands, take what one wants and damn the consequences?'

'Yes,' said Phyllis, uncertainly. 'Please smoke again, Mr Moon, if that's what you mean.'

'I believe that too,' I sighed. 'And I never do it.'

'Why not, Mr Moon?' said Phyllis, more easily.

'Here lies Lord Badger, who disgraced his
  clan.
With all his faults he was a gentleman,'

I murmured. 'I wonder what it feels like,' I
continued.
'Being a gentleman, Mr Moon?'
'Damning the consequences.'
'I can't imagine,' said Phyllis, looking as if
she could never damn a fly.
'It would be rather fun to try,' I said. 'A
pleasant occupation for a Last Day.'
'It would be a pity to spoil your last day,
Mr Moon.'
'True. But one can always pretend, Miss
Fair. For example, one might pretend that
we were going to elope, Miss Fair. Tonight,
Miss Fair. And study our sensations during
the day.'
'There's Mary,' said Phyllis, looking up at
the windows.
'Think what pleasure it would give to
Mary,' I said.
'That's very true,' said Phyllis, twinkling.
'Well, Mr Moon, I don't mind pretending
that. As long as it's only pretend.'
'We should take the midnight train to
Paris,' I mused. 'Paris and the Italian Lakes.
All for Love and the World well Lost. It will

be more realistic perhaps if we actually take the tickets.'

'Rather expensive, Mr Moon, if we don't use them.'

'We can always get the money back, Miss Fair.'

'Very well. And do I pretend to pack, Mr Moon?'

'I think not. We go off suddenly – after a maddening dance. At the "Thames", perhaps. And you buy a new trousseau in Paris.'

'Hardly a trousseau, Mr Moon.'

'Oh, well!'

'What fun!' said Phyllis. 'I feel desperately wicked already. Paris and the Italian Lakes! Meanwhile, Mr Moon, let's bathe in the Thames!'

'Not yet,' I said lazily, taking out a pipe.

'You seem to forget, John,' said Phyllis, imperiously, 'I am now your – your–'

'My what, Phyllis?'

'I am in command, Mr Moon.'

We bathed.

We bathed. And we sat about. And we lunched. And we sat about. And we bathed. And we played a little tennis. I said a graceful goodbye to my hostess. And Mary sent many affectionate messages to Angela, whom she said she had seen several times recently, a little to my surprise. And in the cool of the evening, the tide favouring, the west wind behind us, we slipped down the river in the The *White Witch* to London.

It was not great sailing. There was no spice of danger in it, except that Phyllis insisted on holding the tiller (she had been insisting most of the day, I reflected), and that I could look at nothing else, Phyllis being in her champagne dancing-frock and a cloak, with nothing on her head. But it was the perfect motion for the gentle ending of a summer's day. Without effort, without sound, but for the enchanting lisp and chuckle at the bows, borne by the wind and the water of heaven, scorning the aid of machines or men, we glided down the river to London, a river splashed with rose and purple as the sun fell, a London golden like the temples of the East.

From Mortlake to the mouth of the Wandle we did not speak.

Then 'Lovely!' Phyllis sighed. 'But you know, Mr Moon, we shan't get this in Paris. Nor yet in the Italian Lakes.'

'All for Love,' I murmured.

At Westminster we landed, took a taxi, and after a mild protest from Phyllis, booked our tickets to the Continent.

167

Then we re-embarked and travelled on to the Thames Club. A large crowd gathered on Westminster Bridge, and there was a good deal of cheering and waving as we sailed away.

'The dears!' said Phyllis gaily, 'they little know what we've been doing. What would they do if they did, do you think?'

'We should be stoned,' I said.

'The brutes!' said Phyllis.

'Dear *White Witch*,' she said, as we tied her up for the last time at the 'Thames' steps. 'What will you do without her?'

'All for Love,' I murmured. 'I shall give her to Mr Smith. A fair exchange.'

We dined in the courtyard. There were no other diners, and after dinner the moon came up.

The waiters having withdrawn, I sang again in my low sweet tenor:

'So we'll go no more a-roving
So late into the night–

and the rest.

And a great mist of sentiment rose up out of the river.

'Charming,' Phyllis murmured. 'But it's not so suitable now, is it – because of course we *are* going a-roving, aren't we?'

'Of course.'

'Do you know, Mr Moon,' said Phyllis, reflectively, 'now that we've taken this great decision, now that I'm going to be with you forever and ever – I don't seem to like you so much as I did.'

'That's very curious,' I said.

'It seems to spoil things somehow,' said Phyllis.

'That's curious, too.'

'How strange it will be to see you every day, John, instead of only now and then!'

'But how delightful!' I murmured.

'On the contrary–'

'I beg your pardon?'

'On the other hand, I mean – I have never seen you yet when you weren't on your best behaviour. I suppose I shall now,' said Phyllis. 'Are you nice in the home, John?'

'Except after breakfast,' I said. 'And before breakfast,' I added.

'That doesn't leave much of the day, Mr Moon. And then,' she pursued, 'seeing you every day, John, there will be nothing to look forward to.'

'There will be plenty to look back at,' I remarked.

'True,' said Phyllis, with a sigh, gazing

across the river. 'It's rather sad to think that we shall never be able to come to this jolly place again.'

'Why not, Phyllis?'

'Well, we shall be – what's the word? – ostracized, shan't we? Like the people in novels.'

'Who cares?' I said, intensely. 'A great passion is the pinnacle of life; and from that pinnacle we will look down upon the guilty world, not they on us. Like people in novels. Are there not dancing-halls in Italy, my dear?'

'I don't want to dance with Italians,' said Phyllis.

'You won't,' I said, strongly.

'I don't think you're going to be at all nice in the home, Mr Moon.'

'And then, my dear,' I went on, earnestly, 'think of it! No more concealment, no more furtive meetings – isn't that worth a sacrifice?'

'I can't remember that we've *had* any furtive meetings, John. I've always thought they must be rather fun.'

'I don't believe you've *read* any novels,' I said, disgustedly.

'Don't think I'm regretting our decision, John,' said Phyllis. 'I shall love being ostracized by Mary. Hullo, there's Gordon!'

'Oh, Lord!' I replied, tersely.

Dancers were beginning to arrive, and with them, of course, the inevitable Mr Smith – Smith and Lettice Trout!

'You won't mind my dancing with Gordon once or twice, John?' said Phyllis, with mischief in her eye. 'You see, now that we're eloping, you have a life of me before you – but it's Gordon's last night, isn't it?'

'Of course,' I said. 'But you won't forget that our train goes at midnight?'

'Of course not, Mr Moon.'

At ten minutes to twelve I watched them dancing for the third time, magically graceful, magically at one. And it may be that I sighed; for I shall never dance like Mr Smith. I should never be magically at one with Phyllis, though I danced with her for life.

Phyllis joined me in the courtyard at the end, flushed and glowing, and her eyes shining.

'Well, Mr Moon,' she said, brightly, 'is it time to go? I'm so excited.'

I pointed up the river to a line of light flickering across a bridge.

'The midnight train,' I said. 'I'll take you home instead.'

'Oh, dear, we've missed it!' said Phyllis. 'Won't Mary be disappointed?'

'Disappointed? How, Miss Fair?'

'Well, of course, I gave her just the tiniest hint, Mr Moon.'

'The deuce you did!' I said.

'The end of a perfect day,' said Phyllis, later, looking down like an angel from her front door. 'I hope it *has* been perfect, John.'

'It has, Phyllis,' I sighed.

'And I hope it was the right end,' she said, demurely.

'I expect it was.

'You weren't serious?' she said, anxiously. 'You *were* pretending?'

'Of course,' I said. 'But it was worth pretending.'

'I don't know. I like you much better now.'

'Exactly,' I said, taking her two hands. 'It was worth it – for that.'

'Well, goodbye, John. Virtue is its own reward, remember.'

'But sometimes,' I said, looking up and down the street, 'it is as well to humour it with something more, a little testimonial, shall we say–'

'Well, just the tiniest, perhaps,' said Phyllis, coming down a step. 'Goodbye, John.'

And in the morning I took the train to my house.

I opened the front door and put my foot upon a letter. It was from Angela; and it began:

'DEAR ROBIN,
 'You will not find me at home...'

I gasped. Somehow I had never thought of that. It went on:

'I am sorry to have to tell you that I have been compelled to institute proceedings for a divorce... You and Phyllis...'

I gasped a second time.

CHAPTER 11

The Difference

It is curious that while the Birth Rate and the Death Rate continue to fall the Marriage Rate continues to rise. It is curious that while much is said and written about the Divorces which take place in our land, little is said about the Divorces which do not take place. Indeed, few people realize how numerous they are. This, of course, is the fault of Literature and the Drama. For a man can no more make a play out of a happy marriage than he can make an omelette without breaking eggs.

The average number of marriages in the United Kingdom every year is

400,000, odd.

The average number of divorces in the United Kingdom is

1,000, odd.

And since on the average it takes from four to five years to bring a given couple to the blessed state of divorce the true statistical proportion of divorce to marriage may be said to be not 1 in 400, but 1 in 2,000.

This is not at all bad. But I do not remember a play in which these figures were very clearly illustrated.

There would be even more marriages, I think, and even fewer divorces, if they were all managed like mine.

Nevertheless, it is even now an occasional complaint of my dear wife Angela's that I made fun of her petition for divorce. Had it ever come to court she might have had reason to complain; for failure of any kind means so much in the theatrical profession; and if she should ever want to act again it would no doubt tell against her if she had once brought an unsuccessful suit for divorce. But I remind her always that I meant no disrespect to her, for I never for a moment believed that she had very much to do with it.

Most of the misfortunes of women are attributed to men; but if only women would leave each other alone, how much happier everyone would be! Angela's trouble, of course, was entirely due to the kindly promptings of poor Mary Banbury, inflamed by the twin unselfish motives of busyness and revenge. Revenge? I hate to strike a melodramatic note in an affair so laughable; but there is no doubt that, from that far-off night at Boom's, Mary had never for a moment forgotten that it was Phyllis and I who found her dancing with the policeman, and that it was I who saw what happened at the Dark End. What she did forget was my chivalrous rescue of her from the consequences of her skittishness, and our discreet silence afterwards. But there it is – she was determined in some way to see me discomfited; and no doubt we were foolish not to take her seriously. To be fair to the poor creature, I fancy her schemes ran away with her and took her farther than she intended. As for Angela, I could not blame her. Those innocent adventures of which you have read, without a thought of evil, may well have had a black look when assembled into one story and presented by an artist like Mary. I could see her standing over Angela while that letter was written. And since I had her to thank for the filing of Angela's petition, I resolved that she should assist in removing it from the file.

My first reaction was to call a Conference. Since Mary knew all about my private affairs I took it they were now public property, and there could be no harm in a frank discussion at a semi-public meeting.

I drafted what the politicians call a Three-Lined-Whip:

MARRIAGE (AND DIVORCE) OF MR AND MRS MOON

There will be a discussion of the above at The Shingles, Chelsea, on Friday next, at 12 noon, when serious allegations will be made, and a division of opinion is certain.
<u>*Your attendance is essential.*</u>

I typed this out and sent a copy to Angela, to Phyllis, to Major Trevor, and to Mary Banbury. I nearly sent one to Mr Smith, but decided to let him off. Angela's whip I marked 11.30 a.m.

On Wednesday I rang up Phyllis and had some serious words with her. Then I rang up Mary Banbury.

'Hullo!' I said. 'Good afternoon, Mrs Banbury. You've been butting in, I hear.'

'I've only done my duty,' she said, stiffly. 'What's this nonsense you've sent me? It's time you were serious, Mr Moon.'

'On the contrary,' I said, 'it's taking these things seriously that keeps the lawyers busy. By the way, Mary, can you tell me what Major Trevor's been doing the last few weeks?'

'How should I know?'

'You know everything,' I said, respectfully.

Along the wires I could somehow feel the passage of a reluctant, satisfied purr.

'It's nothing to do with me,' she said.

'It's your duty,' I said. 'Could you tell me, for example, which day it was he asked Angela to run away with him?'

'I can't tell you anything.'

'Oh!' I said, and there was a short pause. 'You're coming on Friday, of course?'

'Certainly not.'

'That's a pity, Mrs Banbury. Serious allegations will be made, you know.'

I paused again. No sound was heard.

'In that case I'd better send the whip to Jack instead. I thought perhaps you'd rather come yourself.'

No sound was heard.

'On the other hand,' I said, 'I *might* be able to let you off altogether. I hate to mention it,' I went on, 'but does Jack know about the policeman?'

'Why are you such a beast?' said the lady, surprisingly.

'I'm only doing my duty,' I said, sadly. '*Does* Jack know—'

'No.'

'In that case – I repeat – do you know anything about Major Trevor? Nothing unpleasant, you understand, but anything in the nature of a general discussion on elopements, mutual glances at the Opera, prolonged handshakes, exceptional politeness, joint visits to dressmakers, joint attendance at matinées, unsigned notes or affectionate trunk calls? Anything of that nature?'

'I shall be alone at tea-time,' said Mrs Banbury at last.

'Very well,' I said, and rang off.

On the Friday morning Angela arrived first, as I had arranged. She came in jauntily, looking her very best, and wearing a copy of her 'going-away' hat – the rogue! Ten seconds later we were wrapped, as the novelists say, in a fond embrace.

'Oh, dear!' she sighed, disengaging herself at last, 'I'm so happy, Robin. I knew it couldn't be true.' And she was so overjoyed that she began to cry.

'What couldn't be true?' I asked, in the first pause.

'What they all s-s-said about you,' she sobbed.

'Who are they all?'

'Well, Mary, chiefly,' she said, drying her eyes.

'Then of course it wasn't true. And may I observe,' I said, severely, 'that in listening to anything that anybody said you have broken Rule 4 of the Regulations for the Conduct of a Holiday Moon. Any indiscretions, as you know, are reported by the party concerned at the end of the Moon. In the normal course I should now give you the true account of the various episodes of which "they all" have told you. As it is, I shan't tell you anything.'

'Oh, well,' said Angela, clinging; 'it doesn't matter now. I never believed it.'

'Then why,' I began, 'did you act as if–' But I remembered that I was speaking to a woman.

'Then you'll take the little petition off the file?' I said instead.

'The what?' she said, as if she had for-gotten all about it.

'The petition, my dearest.'

'Oh, yes, Robin, of course! That's all right,'

said Angela, clinging still more. 'Only –
only–'

'Only what?'

'Only I *do* think it would be better if you
didn't see Phyllis any more.'

Angela peeped up at me under her hat as
she said this, her eyes exceedingly bright
and cunning, like a naughty bird's.

'Well, I'm–' I replied, with a sigh. 'Then
you *are* jealous?'

'Jealous!' she cried, and stopped clinging.
'How absurd you are! No, Robin, it's not
that. But she isn't – she isn't *worthy* of you.
You're too good for her. That's all.'

'That's nonsense,' I replied, I regret to say.

'I can't think *what* you see in her.'

'What do you see in Major Trevor?' I
asked, gently.

'That's different,' said Angela.

'How?'

'You can't compare him and Phyllis,' said
Angela, who thinks, like many women, that
to defend an unreasonable proposition she
has only to say it again in a different way.
'Bim's just a friend,' she added.

'What's Phyllis, then?'

'She's different,' said Angela, but this time
rashly developed the proposition. 'You know
perfectly well that Phyllis is only playing

with you. Bim's *fond* of me. He's one of my oldest friends. He'd do anything for me.'

'Would he?' I wondered, musing.

'I do think you might be nice,' said the wicked creature, 'after I've forgiven you.'

'Will you give up seeing Bim,' I said, ignoring the infamous implication, 'if I give up seeing Phyllis?'

'Why should I?' said Angela, threatening to cry. 'I tell you he's d-d-different. Will you give up Phyllis if I for-g-give you?'

'No,' I said, kissing the wretch. 'It wouldn't be good for you. It's a matter of principle.'

'It's just like you,' she said, hiding her face, 'to sp-poil it all. Why can't you be nice to me – after all these weeks?'

'Why should I be nasty to Phyllis,' I said, 'after all these years?'

'I'm beginning to think,' said Angela, 'that it *is* true, after all.' And she burst into tears.

A woman in tears is like a wet Sunday in London: it makes a man question the supremacy of Reason. I wavered, as usual; but principle prevailed.

'In that case,' I said, with a sigh, 'we'd better get on with these divorces.'

At that moment the front doorbell rang, and I stepped into the hall. Phyllis had arrived. I took her into the smoking-room and gave her a few instructions. I did not see why she should begin the Conference at a disadvantage.

The Major arrived a minute later. I had arranged four chairs in the drawing-room, committee-wise, two pairs facing each other.

'Will you sit there, Major?' I said gravely, and I motioned him to a seat next to Angela.

'Thanks,' said the Major, with a frightened glance about the room; and he sat down stiffly, as if at an inquest. Angela gave him one look, and continued to cry quietly.

Then I went out and led in Phyllis, leaning on my arm. Phyllis was quite broken-up. Her face was pale; she wore a black dress and a large black hat, and she too was weeping; not noisily, but bitterly – just bitterly. We took the two remaining chairs. When Angela saw that Phyllis was crying, she began drying her eyes.

I cleared my throat.

'Now, sir,' said the Major, 'may we ask the meaning of this foolery?'

I fixed the Major with my eye, in the manner of a fashionable KC.

'Take your mind back to the 14th of June, Major Trevor,' I said, sharply.

The Major's glance wavered under this attack and he made an inarticulate stammering sound.

'Did you on that day put through a telephone call from Carlisle to London, Major Trevor?'

'I may have,' stammered the Major, 'but what the devil–'

'Keep cool, Major,' I said kindly. 'Take your time. And that, I believe, was in order to enjoy a private conversation with Mrs Moon?'

'Certainly,' said he, defiantly. 'Have you any objection?'

'None whatever. And was the cost of this message about three shillings and ninepence?'

'Very likely.'

'A large sum of money for a military man to spend on a mere conversation?'

'No.'

'Exactly. And would it be fair to say, Major Trevor, that in the past four weeks you have attended at least three charity matinées in company with Mrs Moon?'

'Certainly,' said the Major, easily mystified, but greatly relieved, I felt.

'And have you until this month, in the whole course of your career, attended a single charity matinée before?'

'N-no,' said the Major, doubtfully. 'I'm a busy man. But what's all this to–'

'Precisely, Major. And do you in correspondence with Mrs Moon habitually sign yourself "yours ever"?'

'Oh, well,' said the Major, smiling, 'we're very old friends.'

'Exactly. And have you, on any occasion, in bidding her farewell, retained possession of her hand for a longer period than is essential or customary at a formal parting?'

'My dear sir–' the Major began, feebly.

'Exactly, Major. Now let me take you back to the night of the 29th of June. Did you, or did you not, on that night, in the small conservatory at Lady Maud July's, invite Mrs Moon to accompany you to Northern Italy?'

'Look here!' the Major spluttered. 'You've no right – you're going too far, Moon.'

'I'm afraid I must ask you for an answer,' I said gravely.

'I decline to be questioned in this way,' said he, uncomfortably, with a glance at Angela. Then, 'No,' he said, 'I didn't.'

'Oh, Bim!' said Angela, reproachfully. 'You know you always do.'

The Major looked at her; then rose with

decision from his seat, ejaculating the words, 'Look here–'

'Sit down, Major,' I said, soothingly. 'I won't press the question. At any rate, I may take it you have, like other sensible men, an admiration for my wife that amounts at times, to something like affection?'

'Ye – es,' said the Major, cautiously. 'You might say that, I suppose.'

'And there is little doubt, Major, that you would make her happier than I do?'

'I should be sorry to think I couldn't do that,' said the Major, warmly.

'Take her, then,' I said, rising. 'She is yours.'

'I beg your pardon,' said the Major, recoiling.

'Take her I say. Marry her.'

'*Marry her!* You're mad.'

'Not immediately, of course,' I said. 'But my wife, I understand, proposes to divorce me. I, on the other hand, propose to divorce her. The principal evidence against her we have just heard. Similar evidence – almost exactly similar evidence – is available against myself, and will be furnished on demand. Most of it will be presented by a Mrs Banbury. At first sight there may be difficulties on both sides, but any competent

KC will be able to work up the material into a damning case. In less than a year we should both be free.'

'Don't talk such nonsense, Robin,' said Angela.

'Miss Fair, I believe,' I continued, 'is ready and anxious to marry me when it is all over. Am I right, Miss Fair?'

I turned to Phyllis, who hung her head and murmured 'Yes,' with a pathetic little sniff. 'I'd go to the ends of the earth with you,' she said, with a tremor in her voice.

'Thank you,' I said, much moved. 'But before I agree to this change in our relations, I should wish to be certain that my dear wife Angela was to be in safe and competent hands. There is no man, Major–'

'One moment, Robin,' said Angela. 'I want to tell you something.'

'In a minute, my dear. There is no man, Major,' I continued, 'to whom I would more confidently entrust my wife than yourself.' The Major bowed stiffly. 'As a soldier, it is true, you would not be able to give so much time to her as I should wish, but after the proceedings in court you will probably find it convenient to leave the Army, so that that objection may be waived. May I ask if you are given to reading in bed, Major, or reading at meals?'

'Look here–!' said the Major, bouncing up again.

'Sit down, please. Both, I imagine? As a bachelor, both undoubtedly. And both these practices I must ask you to abandon. A wife, at meal-times at least, must be entertained, and reading in bed keeps Angela awake. Then as to matinées. Three matinées in a month is not at all bad for an outsider, Major, but you will be expected to do better than that when you are married. Then there are flower-shows, picture galleries, At Homes, and concerts. And I must particularly request that you take no pleasure in any female society but that of my wife, for this annoys her–'

'Look here, I've had enough of this,' said the Major, rising finally. 'Goodbye, Mrs Moon. And as for you, sir–'

'One moment, Major,' I said, astonished. 'Am I to understand, then, that you *refuse* to marry my wife?'

'You may understand what the devil you please,' said the soldier, unpardonably. 'Now let me pass.'

'Can it be possible, Major,' I said, as one stupefied, 'that all this time you have been merely *playing* with my wife, fostering an affection which you were not prepared to satisfy and nourish with your life? And only this morning' – I sighed – 'she was saying that there was nothing you would not do for her. There is a word, Major, in frequent use at music-halls and among the vulgar, a common word unworthy to describe a delightful, pleasant, though doubtless unproductive form of human intercourse. The word is *flirt*. That word belongs to the vulgar, and I would not utter it of you. But there is a better word. Can it be possible, Major, that you have been merely *dallying*? Oh, *Major!*'

'Come outside!' roared the Major; and, shaking his fist, he pushed past us to the door.

'Bim!' cried Angela. 'Hi! Stop!' And the Major stopped in the doorway.

'I've been trying to tell you, Robin,' she said – 'only you will talk so much – that it's all a mistake. I haven't done anything about a divorce. I never thought of it. I never intended–'

'Pardon my absurd curiosity, my dear,' I said; 'but in that case, can you tell me why you wrote me a letter about it? I fancy you said you'd already filed the petition.'

'It was Mary,' said Angela. 'I had to get her out of the house somehow. And that was the only way.'

'A very reasonable explanation,' I said. 'But in that case perhaps we had better all kiss and be friends.'

So saying, I kissed Angela. And Phyllis and Angela fell on each other's necks, and began crying again. Meanwhile, I held out my hand to the Major.

'*Pax!*' I said; 'and while the ladies are refreshing themselves after their kind, why don't you come downstairs and take a loving-cup with me?'

The Major looked for a moment as if he would eat me, but decided to drink instead. We shook hands.

When Phyllis left (with the Major) the situation was very easy, and there was more kissing. Indeed, the friendliness of the ladies had all the air of a combination against Man. Angela pulled Phyllis back at the last moment, and murmured naughtily, 'By the way, Phyllis, would you *really* have married him?'

Phyllis gave me a quizzical glance, then whispered something in Angela's ear.

'Just what I thought,' said Angela, nodding wisely; and from the pleased expression on her face I could guess the *kind* of remark that Phyllis had made.

The little pig!

'So *there*,' said Angela, a little meaning-lessly, as we shut the door behind them. But I knew what she meant.

'I told you this morning,' I said, 'that they were just the same.'

CHAPTER 12

The Beginning Of The End

Jean Renton and Stephen Trout were married in Sussex, at the parish church of Shambles, and Phyllis, by a very old arrangement, was chief bridesmaid. I will not say that Mr Renton, Colonel Bungay, and other residents of Shambles, were wholly happy about the arrangement. It was pointed out that Stephen and Phyllis were once engaged, and therefore should not, in public, at any rate, confess that they were on speaking terms. But most of us thought that it was a happy gesture by all concerned.

Angela refused to come, for the absurd reason that weddings made her feel unhappy.

The only train of the day deposited the guests from London in the churchyard, as usual, about half an hour before the ceremony. We stood there, chatting stiffly among the gravestones; and it struck me how suitable we were dressed for our surroundings. It was a fine, bright day, and from the churchyard you had a wide, smiling view over the Weald to the dark blue sweep of the Downs beyond. The trees were still green and fresh; birds sang; there was a joy in the air. And we were gathered there to celebrate the happiest day in the lives of two young people. Or so, at least, the poets have agreed to say.

And we were dressed as we should have been dressed to see the same young people cremated. But for Father Trout's white spats, the while 'slip' of Colonel Bungay, and an occasional buttonhole, we men were arrayed exactly as we should have been arrayed for a funeral; most of the women wore black; and Jean, when she appeared, wore a garment extremely like a shroud. Tulle, I fancy. Or maybe taffeta.

Such thoughts as these oppressed my spirit during the service. God knows, I would not pretend that it is not a serious thing to be married; the marriage ritual excellently asserts the solemnity of the contract; and so tremendous is the atmosphere of awe surrounding them that I suppose it is too much to expect the bride and bridegroom to look as if they enjoyed the prospect before them. Jean whispered her 'I will,' poor thing, in the accents of a Christian martyr consenting to be burned alive; and Stephen as if he had been condemned to do the burning. The parson did his part in a voice of doom. A marriage, in theory, I suppose, is the grand beginning of things; but no one can be present at an English wedding without the sensation that it is the end of everything.

Perhaps it is. From where I stood (between two old ladies in black satin and jet) I could occasionally see Phyllis Fair's head and the back of her neck. The 'note' of the bridesmaid's dresses was gold, and she had some kind of a green and gold fillet round her head. She was being very efficient and motherly with two infant bridesmaids, who stood on the bride's train and made ridiculous remarks. She, too, perhaps, would soon be loving, honouring, and obeying. Perhaps a mother. She too would be finished.

I did not think much about the bride and bridegroom. One doesn't – at a wedding. Husbands think about their own wives; and the bachelors think about the bridesmaids. To a certain extent I did both.

One thinks of odd, far, silly things. 'With all my worldly goods I thee endow,' said somebody far away; and I thought of the National Anti-Profiteering Society, who are promoting a Bill, I have read, to give effect to the principle that every man on marriage shall make over a definite proportion of his wealth to his wife. Admirable, no doubt. But the marriage service must then be amended to: 'With 40 per cent of my worldly goods I thee endow, or such other percentage as Parliament shall from time to time determine...'

We sang a sad psalm.

Phyllis, I reflected, was once engaged to Stephen Trout. It might have been her wedding today.

The solemn vows are spoken, their fulfilment is a matter for the future. But *now* – surely – there should be song and dance, feasting and revelry, something at least to give expression to the old-fashioned notion that a marriage is a joyful thing. But this, I know, can scarce be done at half-past three in the afternoon.

What happened was that we gathered in and about a large marquee on a wet lawn. I shook hands with the bride and bridegroom, and moved about among the chattering crowd, nibbling sandwiches and sugar-cakes, and talking about rain.

In the *Rime of the Ancient Mariner* it is written:

The Bridegroom's doors are opened wide,
And I am next of kin,

> The guests are met, the feast is set,
> May'st hear the merry din.

In the marquee there was a din, indeed; but none could call it merry. I saw Phyllis flitting about polite and charming, and she indeed looked gay enough. She seemed very busy, and once, I thought, avoided my eye. And I observed that from time to time she halted and wrote something with a minute pencil in a tiny little golden book.

Presently she came towards me.

'So you've remembered my existence at last?' I remarked.

'Not at all,' said Phyllis. 'I've remembered the existence of champagne.'

I fought a passage between a colonel and a squire and fetched her a glass. Two glasses.

When I returned she was busily writing in the little book again.

'Journalism?' I inquired.

Phyllis looked up, blushing a little. 'Making notes,' she said. 'For a future occasion.'

'Is somebody going to die?'

Phyllis looked puzzled.

'I thought perhaps the occasion was a burial. You might pick up some very useful tips this afternoon. I should certainly have the same parson. And, speaking for myself,

I shall wear the same clothes.'

'You may not be there, Mr Moon. It's a wedding.'

'Whose wedding, Miss Fair?'

'Oh, anybody's! It might be mine.'

'I shall certainly be there.'

'You may not be asked, Mr Moon.'

I looked over her shoulder and read, with difficulty, 'NO SQUASHY BUNS! – CAN'T BE EATEN STANDING – CHAIRS IN MARQUEE – LEMON SQUASH – NOSEGAYS FOR IN-FANTILE BRIDESMAIDS–'

'Have you made any note about the bride-groom?' I asked, and added a little wickedly, 'Something on the lines of Stephen, I suppose?'

Phyllis, I repeat, was once engaged to Stephen.

'Not at all,' said Phyllis, and pouted with her nose, as rabbits do.

'Whoever it is,' I murmured, 'I shall be the best man, Miss Fair.'

'Whoever it is,' said Phyllis, 'I hope you won't give me away, Mr Moon.'

'Well, well,' I sighed, 'I was right, after all. Somebody *is* going to die.'

'Who, John?'

'The bride,' I said, 'at this wedding you speak of. Poor Jean!' And I sighed again.

'*Poor* Jean, Mr Moon? She has achieved the greatest ambition of a woman's life.'

'To achieve your greatest ambition at the age of twenty-four *is* death. Think of it,' I went on earnestly. 'Tonight, of all the fine young men who know and admire her, not one will give her a second thought. No one will say to himself, "Shall I ask Jean to dance with me, or Kate, or Phyllis?" They will say, "Shall I ask Kate or Phyllis?" The name of Jean Renton will be wiped tonight from twenty invisible slates.'

'If you mean Kate Manners,' said Phyllis, a little warmly, 'no man of any sense would ask himself such a question.'

'I meant any, Phyllis,' I said hastily. 'I know several myself.'

'Oh,' said she. 'Well, you're a little depressing, Mr Moon. Wouldn't you be interested in me any more if I was married?'

'Not to the same extent, Miss Fair. It wouldn't be right.'

'It isn't right *now*, Mr Moon. And I think you're wrong about marriage,' she said, in a wise old way.

'Look about you,' I said. 'You may have observed that everyone is talking about love-affairs. No one is talking about this National Anti-Profiteering Society, who are promoting a Bill, I have read, to give effect to the principle that every man on marriage shall make over a definite proportion of his wealth to his wife. Admirable, no doubt. But the marriage service must be amended to: me? As a bachelor, both undoubtedly. And both these.'

Phyllis looked about her.

'Well? I've considered that. And what's the conclusion, Mr Moon?'

'The conclusion is that a marriage is a dull thing, Miss Fair.'

'When it is celebrated at half-past two in the afternoon, I agree, Mr Moon. The wedding I am thinking of will not be.'

'By the Marriage Act, 1886,' I said, learnedly, 'it must be. Between 8.0 a.m. and 3.0 p.m.'

'By the Marriage Act, 1823,' said Phyllis, coolly, 'one can get a special licence and have it done at any convenient time or place. The girl I am thinking of is going to be married at 7 o'clock on a summer's evening. Everyone in evening dress. Including the bridesmaids, Mr Moon. After the service there is to be a banquet. And after that, dancing. And I dare say Mr Moon will drink too much. Or will it be too dull for him?'

'I'm afraid you've missed the point–' I began.

'Come and see the presents,' said Phyllis.

'You're talking about weddings, Miss Fair. I'm talking about marriages.'

'I'm going to see the presents,' said Phyllis, firmly, moving away. I followed.

We wandered with the crowd round the barbarous display of trophies in the billiard-room, Phyllis making an occasional note in her book.

We passed at least five mustard-pots, sixteen toast racks, and seven cases of dessert-knives, a little tactlessly displayed together on a side table.

'Is there so much dessert in all the world?' I murmured.

Phyllis stopped and made a note.

'I wish you wouldn't do that, Phyllis,' I said.

'Why not, John?'

'It annoys me.'

'Why, Mr Moon?'

'I don't quite know.'

Phyllis looked at me and opened her mouth to speak, as if about to say something sharp. But her eyes softened, and she said nothing.

'The Ancient Egyptians,' I remarked, as we passed on, 'when a personage died, presented him with every kind of domestic article, food and drink – enough to supply him for the whole of the after-life. This, I feel, is a very similar custom.'

'How you do repeat yourself, Mr Moon. Oh, what jolly teacups!' said Phyllis.

'They'll soon be broken,' I said, cheerfully. 'Poor Jean. She'll soon be ordering new ones. And new dishes. And new dessert-knives. New this. And new that. In a year or two they'll all be gone. Only Stephen will remain.'

'I *like* ordering things,' said Phyllis.

'Meals?' I murmured. But Phyllis was eagerly examining a basketful of linen.

'Observe,' I said, 'how *domestic* are the gifts. Each, in some subtle way, suggests settledness, finality, the end of things. Sheets and blankets, not gay embroideries. Blotters, not bangles. All is useful. There is nothing for joy.'

'What would you suggest as a "joyous" present, Mr Moon?'

I had no immediate answer.

'Well, not this undoubtedly ancient grandfather clock,' I said at last. 'Night after night, year after year, Jean will ask Stephen if he has wound up this clock. Night after night Stephen will have forgotten it – or, still more awful, he will have remembered it. Night after night–'

'At any rate, they will always know what time it is,' said Phyllis.

'If you are happy,' I said, 'you do not care what time it is.'

'What time is it now?' said Phyllis, casually.

'Day after day–' I went on. 'Can you imagine a lifetime spent with Stephen?'

'I did once,' said Phyllis, soberly. 'That was the day I broke it off. What time is it, John?'

'Can you imagine a lifetime spent with *anyone*, Phyllis?'

I do not know why I went on in this way. I know very well that it was both discreditable and idle. And so I knew at the time.

'I've tried,' said Phyllis, with a patient air. 'I'm doing so now, Mr Moon. What time is it, please?'

I sighed.

'It's Mr Smith, I suppose?'

'It's Mr Moon,' said Phyllis, gravely. 'But I can't imagine it. I've asked you three times–'

'It's four o'clock,' I said.

'I must go and dress the bride,' said Phyllis, and scurried away.

After we had thrown rice in the faces of the happy pair, and sent them off with that accompaniment of jeers and semi-malicious practical jokes which is considered suitable for such occasions, I wandered out on to the deserted lawn, for my train did not leave for another hour. I paced up and down, thinking even less of the bride and bridegroom than before. And presently Phyllis came out.

'There's one present I don't think you've seen,' she said, a little shyly, and turned invitingly indoors. 'Unless you're in a hurry to go, Mr Moon? I've something to tell you.'

'I don't want to hear it,' I said. 'But you may show me the present.'

We went upstairs to a kind of studio, where was the enormous grand piano which Mrs Renton had given Jean. On the music-stand stood a book of old English songs, such as Phyllis sings.

'Sing me a song, Phyllis,' I said.

'What shall I sing, Mr Moon?' said Phyllis, turning over the pages.

'You might sing "So we'll go no more a-roving," Miss Fair.'

'Oh, dear!' said Phyllis. 'That isn't in the book. Are you feeling sentimental, John?'

'Yes, Phyllis. I like it.'

'So do I, John. But I think it's just as well we didn't elope last June, Mr Moon.'

'Possibly, Miss Fair. But why?'

'You wouldn't be sentimental any more, John; not by this time.'

'Not on the Italian Lakes?'

'Not about me. Men are only sentimental about the things they can't have, Mr Moon.'

'And women, Miss Fair?'

'Women are sentimental about the things they've got. Husbands, for example.'

'That's sentimentality.'

'It's very sensible,' said Phyllis.

'You might sing that,' I said, looking over her shoulder.

'Very well, John. But it isn't a woman's song.'

'It isn't a sensible song, certainly. But it suits you, Phyllis.'

Phyllis sang, 'Oh Mistress Mine, where are you Roaming?' – very soft and sweet and clear. And towards the end of the second verse, a slow faint flush crept over her cheeks.

What is love? 'Tis not hereafter;
Present mirth hath present laughter,
What's to come is still unsure;
In delay there lies no plenty;
Then come kiss me, sweet and twenty!
Youth's a stuff will not endure.

'Thank you, Phyllis,' I said. 'But you rather hurried over the last line but one.'

'There's no one here who is – who is twenty,' said Phyllis, softly, looking at the book.

'Thank you, Phyllis,' I said again.

'It's a beautiful song,' she said.

'It is,' I admitted. 'But is it sensible? What, for example, does it mean?'

'It means,' said Phyllis, hesitating – 'it means – well, I told you I had something to tell you, John.' She paused.

'The important line,' I observed, is *"What's to come is still unsure"*. Which is both sensible and beautiful, I agree, for it contains the whole meaning of life, the delicious pleasures of uncertainty.'

'It's a man's line,' said Phyllis. 'But it goes on, Mr Moon, *"In delay there lies no plenty"*.'

'It goes on, Miss Fair, *"Then come kiss me, sweet and twenty."*.'

'Exactly, Mr Moon,' said Phyllis, coolly, meeting my gaze.

'Exactly. Nothing is said, for example, about marriage. The emphasis is on love.'

'Marriage is implied, Mr Moon. For it finishes, *"Youth's a stuff will not endure"*.'

'Not after marriage, he means.'

'You're very perverse, John.'

'The truth is, it might mean anything. But the important line, I repeat, is *"What's to come is still unsure"*.'

'What I was going to tell you, John, was this–'

'I mustn't miss my train, Phyllis,' I said,

looking at my watch. 'Will you be coming up with me? You could tell me better in the train.'

'I'm sorry, John,' said Phyllis, softly. 'Someone said they'd fetch me in a car.'

'"They", Phyllis?'

'Well, he, John, if you must have it.'

'I suppose I must,' I said.

Just then the door opened, and round it came the head of Mr Smith, looking very twenty, and, I suppose, sweet.

'Hullo!' he said brightly – then shyly, 'Have you told him, Phyllis?'

'I've been trying, Gordon. But he will interrupt.'

'I won't interrupt any more,' I said, and I shook him warmly by the hand. 'I'm very glad. I wish you everything. And now I must go.'

'I'm glad, Phyllis,' I said, taking her hand.

And 'Thank you, John,' said she.

And I suppose I was glad.

I'm sure I was.

I am now.

I cannot answer for the future.

'Goodbye, Miss Fair,' I said.

'Goodbye, Mr Moon.'

The publishers hope that this book has given you enjoyable reading. Large Print Books are especially designed to be as easy to see and hold as possible. If you wish a complete list of our books please ask at your local library or write directly to:

Dales Large Print Books
Magna House, Long Preston,
Skipton, North Yorkshire.
BD23 4ND

This Large Print Book, for people
who cannot read normal print,
is published under the auspices of

THE ULVERSCROFT FOUNDATION

... we hope you have enjoyed this book.
Please think for a moment about those
who have worse eyesight than you ...
and are unable to even read or enjoy
Large Print without great difficulty.

You can help them by sending a
donation, large or small, to:

**The Ulverscroft Foundation,
1, The Green, Bradgate Road,
Anstey, Leicestershire, LE7 7FU,
England.**
or request a copy of our brochure for
more details.

The Foundation will use all donations
to assist those people who are visually
impaired and need special attention
with medical research, diagnosis
and treatment.

Thank you very much for your help.